FROM THE
NANCY DREW FILES

THE CASE: Nancy is determined to put an end to the
reign of terror threatening to cripple New York's
Thanksgiving Day parade, sponsored by Mitchell's
department store.

CONTACT: Aunt Eloise's friend Jill Johnston works
for Mitchell's, and she's in charge of the parade's
preparations.

SUSPECTS: Louis Clark—he's the owner of the department store's major competitor, and his feud
with Mitchell's is as old as it is bitter.

Neil Steem—in years past he was sole manager of
the parade. This year Jill Johnston has been pro-
moted over him.

Howard Langley—he's the patriarch of Mitchell's
and his store is on the brink of bankruptcy. The
parade is nothing but a financial thorn in his side.

COMPLICATIONS: Nancy has a long list of suspects,
and she's checking it twice, but if she doesn't come
up with answers soon, Bess may have to do some
last-minute shopping at Mitchell's . . . for a little
something in prison stripes!

Books in The Nancy Drew Files® Series

The Nancy-Drew Files ™

Case 77

Danger On Parade

Carolyn Keene

AN ARCHWAY PAPERBACK
Published by POCKET BOOKS
New York   London   Toronto   Sydney   Tokyo   Singapore

This book is a work of fiction. Names, characters, places, and incidents are either the product of the author's imagination or are used fictitiously. Any resemblance to actual events or locales or persons, either living or dead, is entirely coincidental.

AN ARCHWAY PAPERBACK *Original*

An Archway Paperback published by
POCKET BOOKS, a division of Simon & Schuster Inc.
1230 Avenue of the Americas, New York, NY 10020

Copyright © 1992 by Simon & Schuster Inc.
Produced by Mega-Books of New York, Inc.

All rights reserved, including the right to reproduce
this book or portions thereof in any form whatsoever.
For information address Pocket Books, 1230 Avenue
of the Americas, New York, NY 10020

ISBN: 0-671-73081-9

First Archway Paperback printing November 1992

10 9 8 7 6 5 4 3 2 1

NANCY DREW, AN ARCHWAY PAPERBACK and colophon
are registered trademarks of Simon & Schuster Inc.

THE NANCY DREW FILES is a trademark
of Simon & Schuster Inc.

Cover art by Tricia Zimic

Printed in the U.S.A.

IL6+

Chapter

One

NANCY, I'd forgotten how huge this store is!" Bess Marvin exclaimed. "Everywhere I look, there's something else I want to try on. And we've only been in the store ten minutes!"

Nancy Drew followed as Bess stepped off the escalator on the fourth floor of a gigantic New York City department store, Mitchell's. All around them were colorful dresses, thick hand-knit sweaters, and other fall fashions.

Nancy had been pleased with her outfit when she'd put it on that morning. The long sweater and black stretch pants emphasized her tall, slender figure, and the green of the sweater set off her reddish blond hair. But she couldn't help being tempted by the store's displays of clothes. "Bess, that would look great on you, with your

1

blond hair and blue eyes," she said, pointing to a blue velvet minidress on a store mannequin.

Bess glanced at the dress, then looked critically at her petite, curvy figure. "It would look even nicer if I lost a few pounds," she said.

"This isn't the week to think about dieting," Nancy said. "Aunt Eloise is making a gigantic Thanksgiving dinner—turkey, stuffing, sweet potatoes, homemade rolls, pumpkin pie—"

Bess covered her ears with her hands. "Stop, Nan. I'm gaining weight just hearing about it!"

Nancy laughed, "Well, it's good we don't have time to try on clothes, then. It's after ten. We're already late to meet Jill," Nancy reminded her.

Nancy and Bess had come to New York to spend the Thanksgiving holiday with Nancy's aunt, Eloise Drew. Eloise's good friend Jill Johnston was in charge of the Mitchell's Thanksgiving Day Parade, one of the biggest in the country. The girls had been thrilled to learn that Jill had invited them to get a behind-the-scenes view of the parade.

As the girls continued up the escalator, they noticed that the hustle and bustle of the floors below gave way to a much quieter office area. "We're supposed to find the employee elevator near the credit office," Nancy explained.

On the sixth floor, they saw a sign with an arrow pointing to the credit office. Next to the office was an elevator marked Employees Only. A guard in a blue suit stood at a podium next to it. When Nancy gave him their names, he checked a list, then smiled at the girls.

"Ms. Johnston's office is on the eighth floor," he told them. He inserted a plastic card into a slot, and the elevator doors opened.

When Nancy and Bess stepped off the elevator on the eighth floor, they found themselves in a reception area furnished with elegant modern furniture. Nancy gave her name to the receptionist, and a few moments later a tall, slender young woman with long brown hair appeared from behind a white door that was almost invisible in the wall behind the reception desk.

"Nancy and Bess?" she inquired. When the girls nodded, she smiled and said, "Hi. I'm Bonnie Braun, Jill's assistant. Jill's on the phone, but you can come on back with me."

The two girls followed Bonnie through the door and down a hallway lined with offices. When they turned a corner, Nancy's eyes widened. They had entered an open work area, and it was a madhouse! All around, people were grabbing files, making phone calls, and shouting back and forth to one another. The atmosphere was informal, with people in jeans working on desktops and on the floor. A large map of the parade route, with a list of the acts that were scheduled to appear, was tacked to the wall next to a row of windows.

3

"Feel free to look around. Jill should be out in a minute," Bonnie said, before hurrying to answer one of the ringing phones.

Bess was already walking over to the list of bands, dancers, and celebrities. "Nancy, come over here. Look! Greg Willow is the grand marshal!"

Nancy went over and looked at the list. She couldn't believe it. She, Bess, and Bess's cousin George Fayne had all been fans of Greg's since his days on the soap opera "Next Door." Now he was the country's hottest young actor and star of the country's number one television show, "Coolidge High."

Bess grabbed Nancy's arm. "I wonder if we'll get to meet him!" She was nearly jumping up and down with excitement.

Nancy was about to answer when someone spoke behind her and Bess.

"Nancy?"

The girls turned to see a tall woman in her forties with wavy chestnut hair. She was wearing a burnt orange wool suit and a cream-colored silk blouse with a chunky goldtone necklace and earrings.

"I'm Jill Johnston," she said warmly. "It's so nice to finally meet you. I'm glad you could come."

"So are we," Nancy said sincerely. She introduced herself and Bess, then said, "Thanks so much for letting us get a look at the preparations for the parade. It looks as if you've got a great list of participants."

Jill nodded proudly. "It's quite impressive this year. All of our interns are going crazy because Greg Willow is the grand marshal."

"I don't blame them!" Bess said, her blue eyes sparkling.

"I apologize for the mess around here," Jill said, "but with Thanksgiving just three days away, things are crazy—"

She turned to a young man with short brown hair who was passing by. "Oh, Dan—hold on a second." Her tone of voice changed, and suddenly she was all business. "I want you to call over to Banderas Stables and make sure everything's okay with the horses for Santa's sleigh. Make sure they can arrive by seven Thursday morning."

The young man nodded and jotted something down on a notepad before walking off. Then Jill turned back to Nancy and Bess.

"The warehouse where we build the floats and store the balloons is in Brooklyn," she explained. "It's about a twenty-minute cab ride from here. Bonnie's calling our car service to take me there now, as a matter of fact. Why don't you come along? The studio is something you really shouldn't miss."

Nancy and Bess exchanged a look. "We'd love to go!" Nancy said.

Five minutes later, the three were settled in the back of a sleek black car. Nancy and Bess took in the sights as the driver made his way through the traffic. Stores selling everything from exotic pets to Chinese herbs lined the street, and crowds of people hurried along the sidewalks.

"No matter how many times we come here, New York City always seems a little more exciting than anywhere else," Nancy said, gazing out the window.

"It's as if the whole city is on fast forward," Bess agreed. She dug into her shoulder bag and pulled out a comb, tissues, matches, and her red sunglasses before finding a pack of gum. She offered some to Nancy and Jill, then tossed her things back in the bag's outside pocket.

They rode through Manhattan, then the driver crossed the East River into Brooklyn. Here the landscape changed from crowded skyscrapers to smaller buildings and stores that had more of a neighborhood feel. Then they entered a warehouse area. The driver stopped the car in front of a huge gray building, and Jill and the girls got out.

The building's entrance had a metal slot next to it. When Jill inserted one end of a card into the slot, the lock clicked open.

"What's that card?" Nancy asked. "The guard at the store's employee elevator used one, too."

Jill laughed as she returned the card to her purse. "Your aunt told me you're quite a detective. I should have known you'd be curious! This is my identification card. Everyone who works at

Mitchell's has one. It also has a magnetic strip that works as a key in the store's restricted areas. The stockrooms and offices require the cards for admittance. So do the parade studio and Mitchell's other warehouses."

As she spoke, Jill led the way down a long hallway. She opened a door at the end of it, revealing an open room that was about the size of a football field.

"Wow!" Bess exclaimed as they stepped inside.

In front of them workers were constructing about a dozen floats. The floats depicted many different themes—from a tropical rain forest to a traditional Thanksgiving setting with Pilgrims and Indians. Rock music was playing, and workers were busy hammering and painting.

"It's great to see everything up close," Nancy commented.

"These are just a few of the floats," Jill explained. "The finished ones are stored in another warehouse nearby."

Jill, Nancy, and Bess wandered toward the far end of the studio, where workers were laying out some enormous balloons and inspecting them. Nancy recognized a famous cartoon cat, its face and whiskers distorted into flat, rubbery folds.

"What's going on over there?" Bess asked, and headed toward a taped-off area where two men in goggles, white suits, and boots were welding together metal rods.

"Bess! Get away from there!" Jill shouted.

7

Bess quickly jumped away—and fell backward over some long metal rods. The contents in the outer section of her bag scattered all over the floor. Red-faced, she quickly stood up, then stooped down and gathered up her things.

Jill ran over, followed by Nancy. "Are you all right?" the older woman asked.

"Other than feeling like a clumsy idiot, you mean?" Bess said. "Yes, I'm fine. But I don't understand. What's wrong with going over there?"

"Those men are working with oxyacetylene torches," Jill explained. "In addition to the danger from the flame, the tanks are explosive. That's why they're off-limits. I don't want anyone getting hurt."

At the far end of the room, Nancy noticed a tall young man with curly blond hair who was wearing corduroy slacks and a striped button-down shirt.

"Hi, Jules," Jill greeted him. "Nancy, Bess, this is Jules Langley. His father, Howard Langley, is the owner of Mitchell's. Mr. Langley bought the store about a year and a half ago."

"Nice to meet you," Jules said, shaking the girls' hands. He waved around the bustling warehouse. "So what do you think? Pretty crazy, eh?"

"We love it!" Nancy told him. "Are you working on the parade, too?"

"A little," Jules said. "But my main responsibility is for the store's exclusive cosmetics lines. I'm in charge of that."

"Sounds like a great job," Bess said. "All the mascara you could ever want!"

"Actually, the lab where we develop and test the cosmetics is in the adjoining warehouse. Would you like a tour?" Jules asked.

Nancy and Bess looked expectantly at Jill. "Go ahead," Jill said, glancing at her watch. "I have some things to take care of. Jules, why don't you bring them back to my office here when you're done."

"You got it," he promised. Jules led the girls back down the hallway. He turned left onto another hallway, then used his ID card to open the door at the end of it.

"Here we are," he announced, ushering the girls through the door and into another warehouse.

Nancy and Bess entered a room that was mostly white and stainless steel. The shelves lining the room contained hundreds of glass containers filled with liquids and creams. A few people were examining slides under microscopes, but they didn't seem to notice the girls and Jules. Through a windowed wall, Nancy could see a network of other connecting lab rooms.

"This lab is where we test all our cosmetic products and develop new ones," Jules explained. He pointed to a table with different-size test tubes and all kinds of powders and liquids on it. "That's where most of our ideas get started. A dash of this, a pinch of that, and presto—a new lipstick color is born!"

Bess's eyes focused on a box of silver tubes sitting on the corner of the table closest to them. "Are those lipstick tubes?"

Jules nodded. "Plum Rose, the newest addition to the line." He picked out two tubes and handed them to Nancy and Bess.

Bess opened the tube and twisted up the pink lipstick. "I love it!" she exclaimed.

"And that's just one of our secrets," Jules said, grinning. He pointed through the glass window to the next room, where men and women in white lab coats worked. "They're working on Mitchell's new signature perfume. I'd take you in, but it's a restricted area."

"Mitchell's is going to have its own fragrance?" Nancy asked.

Jules nodded. "It's called Forever. My nose personally voted for the winning scent," he said. He opened a drawer and took out two tiny glass bottles with Forever printed on them in flowing script. "Here, you two can be among the first to try it."

Bess took her small bottle, opened it, then dabbed the perfume on the inside of her wrist, which she then held up to her nose. "Mmmm," she said. Holding her wrist out to Nancy, she asked, "I love it! What do you think?"

Nancy sniffed the rich, musky fragrance. "Very sophisticated, Bess. Very New York. Could we have one more?" she asked Jules. "Our girlfriend George would love it." George hadn't been able to come to New York because she and her parents were spending Thanksgiving in California.

After handing Nancy another sample, Jules said, "Well, I guess I'd better get you back to Jill."

The girls put the samples into their bags, then the three made their way back to the parade studio. Jules stopped next to an open doorway halfway down the hallway leading to the open workroom. "Here's Jill's office," he said.

"'Bye. Thanks for the tour," Bess told him, following Nancy into the office.

Inside, Jill was perched on the edge of her desk, which was covered with newspaper clippings, schedules, and notices. Filing cabinets lined one wall, and a bulletin board hung beneath the room's two small rectangular windows. Two guys were sitting in folding metal chairs next to the desk.

"Hi," Jill greeted Nancy and Bess. "I want to introduce you to Neil Steem, who works with me in public relations. He's in charge of guest relations for the parade. And with him is—"

The girls' eyes went past the brown-haired man and right to the handsome young man seated next to him.

"Greg Willow!" they both exclaimed at once.

Greg smiled shyly and ran his hand through his jet black hair. He was wearing worn chinos, loafers, and a blue-green rugby shirt that matched his eyes exactly.

"He looks even better in person than he does on TV," Bess whispered to Nancy.

Nancy had to admit to herself that she felt a little weak in the knees. She could hardly believe that Greg Willow was sitting right in front of them.

Greg stood up, flashed his famous smile, and held out his hand. "Well, I can see that you two know me. And you are . . . ?"

Bess just stood there, speechless, so Nancy stepped forward and shook the actor's hand. "Hi. I'm Nancy Drew, and this is Bess Marvin," she said. "We've been fans of yours since you were on 'Next Door.' You must be excited to be the grand marshal of the parade."

She felt that she was babbling, but Greg Willow just smiled again. "I'm really looking forward to it," he told her. "I tell you, though, I never realized how much preparation goes into this parade. It all looks so easy when you're just sitting at home, watching it on TV."

Suddenly Bess sprang to life. "Oh, I know!" she gushed. "It's so exciting to be in on the plans."

As she spoke, Bess moved closer to Greg, her eyes shining. Nancy smiled. Bess definitely had a crush on the actor. Not that Nancy could blame her—he was gorgeous!

Neil Steem spoke up. "It's a lot of work, but—"

He broke off as an explosion rocked the room, sending the bulletin board crashing to the floor. Nancy felt her whole body tense. Before she could even react, the room's two windows shattered, sending flying glass showering down on them!

Chapter
Two

GET DOWN and cover your heads!" Nancy shouted urgently. She dropped to the floor and tucked her head beneath her arms. For a few moments, shattered glass rained down around her. Then everything was quiet.

Finally she uncovered her head and looked up. "Is everyone okay?" she asked, carefully shaking shards of glass from her hair and arms.

Jill was crouched beneath her desk, while Greg, Neil, and Bess were clustered next to the chairs. Jill's eyes were filled with fear as she crawled out and stood up. "Wh-what happened?"

Suddenly screaming voices erupted from the hallway. Footsteps pounded as workers began running past the office toward the exit. "Fire!"

one of them was shouting. Acrid black smoke wafted into the hallway.

"Quick—everyone out!" Nancy shouted.

As Bess, Neil, and Greg hurried past her into the hall, Nancy noticed a small trickle of blood on the palm of Greg's hand.

"That explosion was in the studio," Jill said, hesitating. Her face was ashen and tight with worry. "All those people! The floats and balloons for the parade—" She pressed her lips together in a determined line. "I've got to see if anyone is still inside."

"No! Jill, we have to get out," Nancy said forcefully. "The danger may not be over yet. You could get hurt. We'd better wait for the fire department."

Jill moved reluctantly into the hallway and toward the exit, with Nancy behind her. Workers from the studio streamed past in panic. Nancy winced as she saw a woman holding a workshirt over a bloody gash in her cheek.

When they reached the outside door to the warehouse, Nancy heard sirens in the distance. Everything was in chaos. People were running from three different emergency exits, some of them being helped by others. Billowing clouds of black smoke rose into the air from the roof.

"Oh, no!" Jill exclaimed. She grabbed Neil's arm, and the two of them jumped into action, setting up an area for people who were hurt.

Within minutes, police cars, fire trucks, and ambulances screeched to a halt at the curb. One group of fire fighters jumped down from their trucks, set up their hoses, then ran inside the warehouse with them. Another group went to the back of the warehouse. While the police used yellow plastic ribbons to block off the area, paramedics tended to the wounded, who had gathered near Neil and Jill. Nancy was relieved to see that, although several people had cuts, no one appeared to be seriously injured.

"Greg, you should get that hand checked out," Bess said.

"It's just a little cut from the glass," he said, but Bess grabbed his good hand and led him over to the paramedics.

Nancy frowned as she looked back at the warehouse. How could an explosion just happen out of the blue like that? she wondered. Stepping over to one of the fire fighters, she asked, "Do you know what happened?"

The man shook his head. "It's too soon to tell. We have to get the fire out first."

Nancy was about to ask another question, but her attention was distracted as she saw a familiar blond-haired guy being carried out on a stretcher.

"Jules!" she cried, running over to him. His eyes were closed. As the paramedics lifted him into an ambulance, his blond head turned limply to the side.

"He's unconscious, ma'am," one of the paramedics explained. "Judging from the lump on his head, he must have been hit in the head by some flying debris."

Nancy turned away, a feeling of dread in the pit of her stomach. This was a lot more serious than she had thought. She spotted Jill and Neil talking to the fire marshal, so she hurried over to see if she could find out more about the explosion.

"As far as we can tell, ma'am, the fire had something to do with the acetylene torches," the officer was saying. "But we don't know exactly how it happened yet. The two men working with them are both on their lunch break."

Jill threw her hands into the air. "How much damage has been done? When can we resume work? I have a parade to put on this Thursday, and I need some answers now!" she yelled, obviously upset.

"I'm sure the police and fire fighters are doing all they can," Neil said calmly. He thanked the fire marshal, who walked away.

Nancy stepped up to Jill and Neil. "I'd like to help investigate," she offered. "Something about—"

"No, no," Jill interrupted, waving a hand distractedly in the air. "The police and fire marshal are here, and it's your vacation. You and Bess go off and have some fun," she insisted. "I'll have someone go to a pay phone and call a car service for you." She pulled out her business card, then wrote something on it. "In case you need them, here are the phone numbers and addresses for both the store and the warehouse," Jill said, handing Nancy the card.

Nancy turned as Bess and Greg walked up. "Good as new," Greg announced. He held up his hand to show the square bandage covering his palm.

"Glad to hear it," Neil said. He ran a hand through his brown hair, then looked at Greg, Nancy, and Bess. "Look, Jill and I are going to be here for a while, but there's no reason for you to stick around."

"Well, if you're sure . . ." Greg turned to Bess and Nancy. "I'd love to have you both join me for a late lunch. I'm meeting a friend of mine," he said. "After all this, I think some food is in order."

"Wonderful," Jill said, "then we won't need to call a car service after all."

"Sounds good to me," Bess said to Greg, then looked expectantly at Nancy.

Nancy really wanted to stay with Jill and Neil and find out what had happened. There was something about the explosion that just didn't seem right to her. But Bess's eyes were pleading with her to go with Greg. Besides, how often did she have a chance to have lunch with a TV star?

"All right," she agreed. "Food it is!"

* * *

"I love traveling in style," Bess said a few minutes later. She giggled and sank back into the plush leather seat of Greg's limousine.

Greg smiled at her. "I know it's extravagant, but I have a lot of publicity appearances, and I need to get around quickly," he explained. "I was on 'Good Morning, Manhattan' before I came to the warehouse, and I have two more talk shows scheduled this week. Plus I'm being interviewed by about six different magazines. 'Coolidge High' is really popular right now."

"I don't think it's the show. I think it's you," Bess told him.

"Well, thank you," Greg replied.

Nancy watched the two stare at each other for a brief moment. She didn't have to be a scientist to know that there was some chemistry between Bess and Greg.

"This afternoon I have an interview scheduled with *Young You* magazine," Greg added. A sudden glint appeared in his eyes, and he swiveled his head to look from Bess to Nancy, who were sitting on either side of him. "Hey, why don't you two come along? I'm sure it would be okay."

Bess leaned forward and grinned at Nancy, who nodded. "We'd love to!" Bess replied.

Before long, they arrived at Ipso Facto, a restaurant in midtown Manhattan with a bright red awning above the entrance. Inside, tables covered with white cloths were nestled among decorative pillars and potted plants. Framed art deco posters hung on the walls.

"Rob! How ya doin'?" Greg went over to a young man with handsome chiseled features who was sitting in the rear of the restaurant. He had brown eyes and straight brown hair with long bangs that covered half of his left eye. He was dressed casually in blue jeans and a maroon turtleneck.

"Nancy, that's Nigel from 'Next Door'!" Bess whispered excitedly.

"Nancy and Bess, this is Rob Dunn. We used to be on 'Next Door' together."

"We recognized you from the show," Nancy said as they sat down.

Rob laughed. "It's always great to have fans," he said. He flicked a thumb at Greg. "He's so famous, we even get a guard. The manager promised to keep the autograph seekers away so we can eat in peace," he explained, pointing to a man standing by a nearby pillar.

A waiter dressed in black came over to their table, and after taking a quick look at the menu, they ordered.

"All of this excitement has made me hungry," Bess announced after the waiter left.

"What excitement—meeting us?" Rob asked with a teasing smile.

"Well, that too," Nancy admitted. "But just before we came here, there was an explosion at the Mitchell's parade studio."

20

Rob's smile immediately disappeared. "Is everyone okay?" he asked.

"I was one of the lucky ones," Greg said, holding up his bandaged hand. "Just a cut from some glass."

Nancy briefly told Rob about the explosion. "Jules Langley, the owner's son, was knocked unconscious, and several other people were hurt."

"Jules was hurt? I didn't even know about it. I hope he'll be all right," Bess said. She shook her head in disgust. "I can't believe it. The Mitchell's Thanksgiving Day Parade is supposed to be fun, not dangerous."

"Maybe it was just an accident," Greg said. "But it figures that this year, when I'm grand marshal, something would go wrong."

"I *hope* it was just an accident," Nancy said. "The police and fire department are looking into what caused the explosion right now. Fortunately, most of the floats were in the other warehouse."

She stopped talking as the waiter arrived with their food. As he set her club sandwich in front of her, her stomach growled. With all that had happened, she hadn't realized how hungry she was. She bit into the sandwich, momentarily forgetting about the explosion.

Rob glanced over at the manager, who was still standing by the pillar near their table. "Well, Greg, so far I've counted four girls he's turned away. Maybe you should sign a bunch of napkins and let him give them out."

"Nancy, have you noticed all the girls looking at us? They're *jealous* of us!" Bess added, grinning. "Maybe they'll want *our* autographs."

She took out a pen and signed her napkin "Best Wishes, Bess Marvin" with a heart after her name.

"Forget the fans. I'll take that," Greg said. Grinning at Bess, he slipped the signed napkin into his jacket pocket. Bess looked down at her plate and picked up a french fry, but Nancy noticed that her cheeks were flushed with pleasure.

"So what are you girls up to this afternoon?" Rob asked, after taking a huge swallow of his soft drink.

Nancy and Bess looked at each other. In all the commotion, they hadn't really thought about what they were going to do next.

"Well, we're in midtown. Maybe we should go window shopping on Fifth Avenue," Nancy suggested.

Bess's eyes lit up. "You know me—born to shop! I'm ready whenever you are," she said.

After they finished eating, Greg paid the check, then gave the girls the address of *Young You* magazine, telling them to meet him there at five o'clock. Then he and Rob slipped into the limousine, while Nancy and Bess started walking toward Fifth Avenue.

"Nancy, isn't he great?" Bess asked.

"Greg seems like a really nice guy," Nancy agreed. "I think he likes you."

"You do?" Bess's mouth dropped open. "Are you sure? I mean, could he? He's so famous! Tons of girls are in love with him."

Nancy grinned at her friend. "Well, judging by the way he looks at you, I think he likes you a lot."

Bess let out a sigh. "Every time I look at him I think it's a poster, and then I realize the poster is talking to me."

All of the boy-talk made Nancy think of Ned Nickerson, her longtime boyfriend. As a member of his college football team, he had to get ready for the big Thanksgiving Day game and hadn't been able to come to New York.

"Nancy, look!" Bess exclaimed, stopping short on the sidewalk.

They had arrived at Fifth Avenue, and Bess was staring at the window of a fancy jewelry store. "Do you like that bracelet?" Bess asked, pointing to a gold bracelet studded with diamonds and emeralds. "It's on me—as soon as I make my first million, that is."

The two broke out laughing. As they continued their window shopping, Nancy marveled at the beautiful clothes and shoes. Before long, they arrived at Saks Fifth Avenue, one of New York's most exclusive department stores. Inside, makeup counters of every kind stretched as far as the eye could see. Holly branches and twinkling white lights were already decorating the ceiling, signifying the start of the holiday season.

Bess hesitated near the entrance. "You know I've always loved this store," she said. "But now that we've been behind the scenes at Mitchell's, I feel like a traitor shopping here."

"Me, too," Nancy agreed.

They turned to leave. Right across the street was Rockefeller Center. The plaza area was decorated with branches of colorful fall leaves twisted into artistic shapes.

"Now, *this* is New York," Nancy said as they crossed the street and walked through the plaza. At the far side, they paused at a railing and gazed down at skaters who were gliding along on the ice of the rink below. Music blared from speakers, and the setting sun glinted off the ice.

"Hmm, where are my sunglasses?" Bess rummaged through her bag. Finally she looked up at Nancy. "I think I lost them," she said. "They were my favorites, too."

"Where's the last place you had them?" Nancy asked, flipping up the collar of her coat. As the sun set, the chilly November air suddenly seemed a lot colder.

Bess's brow furrowed into lines of concentration. "I'm not sure," she said. "I know I had them in the cab on the way to the parade studio in Brooklyn. After that I don't remember."

"Maybe you left them there," Nancy said.

"We'll call Jill and ask her to bring them with her when she returns to the store—that is, if they weren't destroyed in the fire."

They watched the skaters for a few more minutes and then found a pay phone on the street corner. Nancy fished in her pocket for the card with Jill's number on it and handed it to Bess, who inserted some change in the pay phone and dialed the number.

"Hi, is Jill Johnston there? This is Bess Marvin," Bess spoke into the receiver. After a short pause, she said, "Hi Jill, it's Bess. I just realized I lost my sunglasses, and I think maybe I left them there. I was wondering if you could—"

Bess stopped speaking. She had a confused expression on her face. "Um, s-sure. I'll be right there."

"Bess, what is it?" Nancy whispered.

Bess slowly hung up the phone. She looked as if she were in shock.

"Bess, is everything okay?" Nancy asked. "What did Jill say?"

"I told her that I left my sunglasses, and then she—I—" Bess broke off and covered her face with her hands. When she finally looked at Nancy, two thin tracks of tears stained her cheeks.

"Nancy, the detectives think the explosion at the warehouse was deliberate." Bess swallowed hard before continuing. "They want to question *me* right away!"

Chapter

Three

NANCY STARED AT BESS in disbelief. "They want to question *you?*" she echoed. "Bess, there has to be a mistake. Are you sure you heard her right?"

"I'm positive," Bess said, obviously distressed. "The police think *I* may have caused the explosion!"

"I'm sure it's all a misunderstanding. We'll straighten it out when we get there," Nancy said, giving Bess a quick hug. "They probably just want to ask if you saw anything odd."

During the taxi ride to Brooklyn, Bess stared silently out the window. When they arrived at the warehouse, Neil and Jill were talking to a heavy-set, gray-haired officer on the sidewalk outside the building. Two younger officers were checking to make sure the police barriers were in place.

Except for two police cars, all the other emergency vehicles had gone. The fire was out, but a terrible smoky smell hung in the air.

"Detective Green, this is Bess Marvin and Nancy Drew," Jill introduced the girls to the older man. Lines of worry were etched into Jill's brow.

"Ms. Marvin?" the detective asked, running a finger over his bushy gray mustache.

When Bess nodded, the detective reached into his pocket and pulled out a plastic bag containing the charred remains of a pair of sunglasses and a book of matches from the River Heights Café. "Are these yours?" he asked.

"Yes," Bess answered slowly. "How did you—?"

"Bess, I told them they were yours. I remembered them from the car ride," Jill explained.

"I—I don't know how you have them," Bess said, looking confused. "They must have fallen out of my bag."

Detective Green gave Bess a dubious look. He stepped over to one of the police cars and returned with a second plastic bag. This one contained a charred red-and-white plastic box with a timer attached. Nancy stared at the box in surprise. It had to be the timer that had been used to set off the explosion!

"Have you ever seen this before?" the detective asked Bess.

"No. Never," Bess replied, shaking her head.

She looked as if she was about to cry. Nancy couldn't remain silent any longer.

"Detective, Bess was with me all day long," she said, stepping forward. "I've known her almost my whole life, and she would never do anything like this." She pointed at the bag with Bess's glasses in it. "Besides, what do Bess's sunglasses have to do with the explosion?"

The detective shot Nancy a glare that said he didn't appreciate her intervention. Neil Steem stepped forward and explained. "They were found lying near the acetylene torches, Nancy," he told her.

"They must have dropped out of Bess's bag when she fell near the tanks earlier," Nancy explained.

The detective jotted a few words in his notepad, then shifted his gaze back to Bess. "Ms. Marvin, why don't you tell me everywhere you've been today?"

Bess took a deep breath, then began retracing her steps from the time she and Nancy had left Eloise Drew's apartment that morning. When she finished, the detective stepped away to confer with the two other police officers. They had finished checking the police barriers and were waiting nearby.

Nancy tried to give Bess an encouraging smile, but Bess merely stared down at her feet.

"Ms. Marvin," Detective Green said, returning to the group, "so far the only evidence we have—and I'll admit it's not much—points to you as the one who set up the explosion. So I'm going to have to ask you not to go back to River Heights just yet."

Bess's face was bright red. Tears streaming down her cheeks, she nodded wordlessly. A moment later, Detective Green gestured to the other officers. After saying goodbye to Jill and Neil, they got into their cars and left.

"Jill, I'm so s-sorry, but I really didn't do anything wrong," Bess stammered, giving Jill a beseeching look.

Jill hesitated for a moment. "I—I know," she finally said, rubbing her temples as if she had a headache. "Look, it's over. I'm sure the police will find out what really happened. Let's try not to think about it." Despite her words, Jill didn't look entirely convinced of Bess's innocence.

"This job's not all fun and games, huh, Jill?" Neil said, patting Jill on the back. "At least there's still enough time to repair the damaged floats and balloons before Thanksgiving."

Nancy turned to gaze at the studio warehouse. "Was there a lot of damage?" she asked.

"Come on. You can see for yourself," Jill said with a sigh. "We were pretty lucky. The fire was put out right away, and the floats were far enough away from the tanks that they only received minor damage. And most of the balloons were at the other warehouse," she explained. She stepped past the police barricades and used her ID card to unlock the outside door, then led the way down the long hallway to the studio.

The group paused inside the studio door to look around. The floor and wall close to the tanks were completely burned. Small yellow caution triangles had been laid out on the floor. Some of the windows had been blown out, leaving shattered glass everywhere, and there was considerable water damage. But farther away from the tanks there was less damage.

Jill pointed to the cat balloon Nancy had seen earlier. Its face was charred, and one paw was nothing more than a large burnt hole.

"Is there any word on how Jules is doing?" Bess asked, her voice barely above a whisper.

"We called the hospital and found out that he's okay, except for a sprained wrist and a slight concussion," Neil answered. "They're keeping him overnight in the hospital for observation."

Glancing at her watch, Nancy realized that it was already a quarter to five. She and Bess were due to meet Greg at *Young You* in just fifteen minutes. Still, she didn't want to leave if Jill needed them. "Jill, is there anything we can do?" Nancy asked.

Jill forced a smile. "No, no. Neil and I can handle it," she said wearily. "I'm sorry I had to call you back, but the police insisted."

Nancy was lost in thought while Jill called them a taxi. She knew that Bess hadn't had anything to do with the explosion, but someone had. Two questions kept nagging at Nancy: Who *was* responsible? And why had they done it?

"I know I'm going to jail," Bess said glumly twenty minutes later. A cab had just let off Nancy and her in front of a brownstone building at Thirty-sixth Street and Seventh Avenue.

"Bess, the police didn't say anything about jail," Nancy said, hesitating outside the building. A brass plate next to the door read Young You. Even though they were a few minutes late, Nancy didn't want to go in when Bess was still so upset.

Bess rubbed at an imaginary spot on her leather jacket. "Once Greg finds out about this, he's never going to like me. He'll think I'm a criminal."

"If he really likes you, he's not going to believe you're a criminal." Nancy pulled a mirror out of her purse and handed it to Bess. "Here. Put on some more of that Plum Rose lipstick. I bet Greg will love it."

"You think so?" Bess asked hopefully. She quickly freshened her makeup, then squared her shoulders and said, "Okay, I'm ready."

Inside, the girls were greeted by a red-haired woman sitting behind the reception desk.

"Hi, we're supposed to meet Greg Willow," Nancy explained to the woman.

"Oh, you must be Nancy and Bess," the receptionist said with a smile. "Come with me." They followed her down a hall lined with framed

31

covers of past issues of *Young You* and knocked lightly on one of the doors. "They're right in here," the receptionist said, pushing the door open.

Greg was sitting on a bright green couch in the office, across from two women. A man with a camera was poised in front of him snapping pictures. Rob Dunn was sitting at a table to the side. Apparently the interview had already started, but Greg stopped speaking and introduced Nancy and Bess to the reporter, Gwen, and the photographer, whose name was Darren.

"Crisis! Crisis!"

Just as Nancy and Bess joined Rob at the table, a woman breezed into the room. "We have a crisis!" she cried, throwing her hands in the air.

"What is it?" Gwen asked. "By the way, this is Cheryl, our beauty editor," she told Greg, Nancy, Rob, and Bess.

"My two models for the make-over spread are stuck in a snowstorm in the Denver airport. The stylists and photographer are waiting for them right now. I have two pages in the February issue to fill, and no models!"

Cheryl stopped speaking and looked at Nancy and Bess. "Who are you?" she asked abruptly.

When the girls introduced themselves, the beauty editor continued to stare at them. "I could hire two other models, but you two look like naturals," Cheryl said. "How would you like a make-over at Salon Salon? Are you available now?"

Nancy and Bess looked at each other. They'd read about Salon Salon in magazines. "Nancy, that's where movie stars get their hair cut!" Bess said, looking excited for the first time since their talk with the police.

"We're definitely available," Nancy told the beauty editor.

"I'll meet you two at the salon when my interview is over," Greg said. "Good luck!"

Salon Salon was located on the fifth floor of Mitchell's, which was just a few blocks away from *Young You*. As they walked over to the store, which was open until nine that night, Cheryl explained that Mitchell's had agreed to do the shoot to promote their new line of cosmetics. She gave them each a *Young You* T-shirt, which she asked them to wear for the shoot.

When they reached the salon, Nancy and Bess were introduced to Ricardo, who ran the salon. After changing into the T-shirts behind a screen that had been set up, the girls posed for some "before" photos, to show the readers what they had started out looking like. Then Ricardo and his staff took over, washing, cutting, and styling the girls' hair. The photographer flashed away, recording each step so the magazine's readers could see the process for themselves.

At first, Nancy felt self-conscious with the

camera clicking away at her. But as she became more involved with watching Ricardo as he cut and set her hair, she forgot all about the photographer.

While Nancy's hair was still twisted up with some spongy pink curlers, a makeup artist began working on her face. A second makeup artist was working on Bess in the next chair. Before long, Cheryl and two assistants set up the white backdrop that the girls were to stand in front of to show off the finished results.

Nancy glanced over at the next chair as Bess's long blond hair was being combed out. The eye shadow and blusher the makeup artist had chosen perfectly complemented Bess's blue eyes and rosy complexion. Bess was smiling at her reflection—she seemed to have completely forgotten about the explosion.

As Ricardo pulled out Nancy's rollers, she turned to look at herself in the mirror. Her hair fell to her shoulders in soft reddish blond waves. The makeup artist had chosen a dusty rose blusher, a blue-gray eye shadow, and a lipstick in a reddish pink. Nancy had to admit that the colors looked great on her, and the white T-shirt set off her face perfectly.

"Voilà!" Ricardo said, running his fingers through Nancy's hair. "Beautiful."

"Okay! Over here for photos of the results and then you're free to go," Cheryl announced, gesturing for the girls to stand in front of the white backdrop.

Just as they got out of the chairs, Greg and Rob walked into the salon. The two young men whistled when they caught sight of Nancy and Bess.

"Who are these two beauties?" Greg asked Rob. "I thought we were meeting Nancy and Bess."

"I don't know, but let's ditch Nancy and Bess and ask these models to dinner instead," Rob answered, grinning.

Cheryl looked back and forth between Nancy and Bess, and Greg and Rob. "Hey! I just had a great idea," she said. "The February issue means Valentine's Day. Why don't you two heartthrobs join the action and pose with Nancy and Bess for some pictures?"

The two guys looked at each other. "Why not?" Greg agreed.

It took only a few minutes for them to change into *Young You* T-shirts. Then the makeup artists dusted a little powder on their faces and combed their hair. The photographer flipped on some music, and the four stepped in front of the white backdrop.

"Okay, just dance. That's it. Smile, turn toward me," the photographer called out.

Nancy swayed to the beat along with the others, while the photographer snapped dozens of pictures. After a few minutes, the photographer looked up from the camera and said, "How about a hug? A group hug."

Nancy felt herself smooshed between Rob and Greg as the four of them pulled together. Before long, the photographer yelled, "That's a wrap!"

"That was fun." Bess giggled as she stepped away from the backdrop.

Cheryl came over from her position behind the photographer and thanked them. "You were great. Give my assistant your addresses, and we'll send you some advance copies."

"Well, now that you look so beautiful, how would you like to accompany me to a dinner party at Café Morelli?" Greg asked Nancy and Bess. "Neil organized it for all the guests of the Mitchell's parade. Rob, you're invited, too," he added.

"I'd like to, but I've got lines to learn," Rob said regretfully. "I'm auditioning for a part in an off-Broadway play," he explained to the girls.

"What about you two?" Greg asked, turning to Nancy and Bess.

"Count me in," Bess quickly answered.

Nancy hesitated. There were only three days until Thanksgiving. If someone was trying to sabotage the parade, she wanted to find out who it was. "I'll meet you there later, okay?" she said. "Right now, I'm going upstairs to see if Jill's around. I want to talk to her about the explosion."

* * *

36

"You can go up, Ms. Drew," the guard at the employees' elevator told Nancy a few minutes later. "In fact, Ms. Johnston says to give you free access from now on."

Nancy rode up to the eighth floor. It was after seven, and the reception desk and open work area were deserted. When she got to Jill's office, Nancy saw that Jill was leaning forward over her desk, rubbing her temples.

"More problems?" Nancy asked gently, sitting down next to the desk.

Jill sighed and looked at Nancy. "Two high school bands just backed out because they don't have the money to fly to New York, and one of the celebrities is sick and might not be able to make it. I don't mind working late, but not when it's all problems!"

Nancy nodded sympathetically. "I hate to bring it up, but have the police or fire department found out anything more from their official investigation of the explosion?"

"Nobody saw anything unusual," Jill replied. "I'm just trying to put it behind me and move on."

Just then the phone rang. Jill looked at Nancy and rolled her eyes before picking up the receiver. "Hello? Yes, this is Jill Johnston."

A look of dread crossed Jill's face. "What!" she exclaimed in a panicked voice. "When did it happen?" After a short pause, Jill said, "I'll be right there. I'm leaving now." Then she hung up the phone and turned to Nancy.

"That was our security office. They just got a call from the security guard at the parade studio," Jill said, slipping her arms into the jacket that was slung over the back of her chair. "Someone broke into the warehouse!"

Chapter
Four

W<small>HAT</small>?" Nancy cried out, astonished.

Jill grabbed her purse and rose to her feet. "I'm not sure of the details, but I have to get over there right away."

"I'll come along," Nancy offered.

Jill's response was a hurried nod as she picked up her phone to call for a car. Five minutes later, the two were speeding toward Brooklyn in the back of a hired black sedan.

"The night security guard said the cosmetics lab was broken into," Jill said, clasping and unclasping her hands in her lap. "I can't believe it! First the explosion and now a break-in."

"Are there guards on duty all the time?" Nancy asked. She didn't recall seeing one there earlier.

Jill shook her head. "Just at night," she replied. "We have a guard posted at the main entrance, and he also patrols the building from time to time."

"At least this time Bess is in the clear," Nancy pointed out. "I was with her all afternoon, and she's with Greg Willow, Neil Steem, and the other parade guests now."

"That's a relief," Jill said, but her voice remained tense.

It wasn't long before they arrived at the warehouse. A police car was already parked in front of the building, and the night guard stood outside the warehouse door. He was talking to one of the younger officers who had been on the scene after the explosion earlier. As Jill and Nancy got out of their car, the guard jogged over to meet them.

"I was making my rounds, and I noticed the outside door to the lab was open," he explained. "I went inside and saw that the inner lab had been broken into, as well. Whoever broke into the cosmetics lab got away, though. He got in through one of the windows that was boarded up after the explosion. Come on, I'll show you. The other officer is inside."

Nancy followed the others down the hallway to the lab door and waited while the guard used his card to let them in. He had closed the door after letting the police in. As Nancy stepped through the doorway, she saw the second officer in the restricted lab looking through drawers. He was wearing thin plastic gloves. The guard let them into the restricted area. Nancy decided to start looking for any clues, trying not to be obvious.

First she examined the lock on the door. There were some fine scratches near the handle. It looked as though the intruder had forced the door open.

Next Nancy gazed around the lab, but nothing seemed to be out of place. Even the explosion hadn't done much damage, although she noticed a crack in the room's glass wall.

She was just turning to give the room another glance, when a white piece of fabric sticking out from beneath one of the steel counters caught her eye. She bent down and saw it was a handkerchief with the initials L.C. monogrammed on it.

"I think I've found something!" Nancy hurried over to where Jill was talking to one of the police officers. She led them back to where she had found the handkerchief. The police officer, whose badge read Rodriguez, stooped, picked up the handkerchief, and put it into a plastic bag.

Nancy turned to Jill. "Do you know anyone who has the initials L.C.?"

"L.C. . . ." Jill echoed, thinking. "No one I can think of. Wait—Louis Clark!" As soon as she said the name, Jill frowned and added, "No, it couldn't be him."

"Who is he?" Nancy inquired.

"He's the owner of Clark's Department Store, Mitchell's biggest competition," Jill explained. "He's tried to undermine us before—planting spies in our marketing department to steal our publicity campaigns, luring exclusive designers

41

away from us . . ." She waved her hand distractedly. "Louis can't stand the parade because it generates so much publicity and goodwill for Mitchell's. But I can't believe he would resort to violence."

Nancy met Jill's sober gaze. "We can't be sure that this break-in and the explosion are related, but I wouldn't be surprised if they were," she said. "And so far Louis Clark is our only suspect. I intend to find out more about him."

The police officer gave Jill and Nancy a disapproving look. "You don't know for sure whose handkerchief this is," he said. "Until you do, I suggest you lay off Louis Clark. Leave this investigation to the police." With that, he turned and joined his partner, who was making out a report by one of the lab tables.

Jill frowned after the officer. "It doesn't sound like the police are going to take a firm stand with Louis," she whispered to Nancy. "Were you serious about pursuing this case?"

Nancy nodded. "The only way to prove that Bess wasn't responsible for that explosion is to find out who was," she explained.

"If you're as good a detective as your aunt says you are, I feel better already," Jill said, smiling at Nancy. "I'll give you any help I can, but please keep this quiet. I'd like to keep this away from the press. Any bad publicity would really hurt the parade."

Suddenly a forceful female voice spoke up

from behind Nancy and Jill. "Okay, Jillie, what trouble are you causing now?"

Nancy turned to see an attractive woman enter the cosmetics lab. Her jet black hair was swept back into a french twist, and she was wearing a stylish navy blue suit with big buttons.

"Hi, Aileen," Jill said. "Aileen Nash, this is Nancy Drew. Aileen is a reporter for Channel Seven news, and she also happens to be my good friend from high school. What are you doing here?"

"I heard about the break-in over my handy-dandy police radio," Aileen explained. "Since I'm covering the parade, I figured I'd better get over here." She tapped a laminated card with her picture on it that was clipped to her lapel. "Thanks to the temporary pass you gave me, the guard let me in."

"This is Aileen's third year covering the parade," Jill explained to Nancy. "She's doing a week-long series of stories about the preparations."

"So what's going on? Explosion this morning, break-in this evening. Is there anything I should know about?" Aileen waved in the direction of the outside door. "By the way, I should warn you there are more reporters out there."

Nancy listened as Jill told her friend all that had happened. "But that's off the record, Aileen," Jill said firmly. "I don't want any of this in your reports on the parade." She started

43

resolutely down the hallway toward the exit. "Now I'll give you and the rest of your colleagues the official version of the story," she said over her shoulder to Aileen.

Nancy followed the two women outside, where a dozen reporters and a handful of cameramen stood poised on the sidewalk. As soon as Jill appeared, the cameramen trained their bright lights on her and started their cameras rolling.

"Hello, everyone. I'm Jill Johnston. I'm in charge of Mitchell's Thanksgiving Day parade," Jill began.

Nancy was impressed by how confident Jill sounded. She didn't reveal any of the worry Nancy knew she must be feeling. Jill went on to say that the guard had reported a break-in when he had seen doors to a restricted area open. She speculated that perhaps the doors weren't working properly due to the explosion.

"What about the explosion?" one of the reporters called out.

"The police are still investigating, but there are no leads yet," Jill answered. "Luckily there were no serious injuries or damage. Any other questions will be taken by my office in the morning. Thank you."

The lights on the cameras clicked off, and the reporters dispersed, murmuring among themselves. From what Nancy could tell, they seemed to accept Jill's explanation.

Jill, Nancy, and Aileen made their way back down the warehouse hallway to Jill's office. The shattered glass had been swept up, Nancy saw, and plywood had been nailed over the windows to keep out the cold. However, the smell of smoke was very strong.

"I almost wish Neil had kept this job another year," Jill said as she collapsed in one of the chairs.

Nancy gave Jill a curious look. "He used to be in charge of the parade?" she asked.

"He had the job for two years," Aileen explained. "This year Jill beat him out for the top position." Raising an eyebrow at Nancy, she added, "Between you and me, I like working with Jill much better. Neil wouldn't even let me into the parade studio—said it would ruin the surprise."

"He actually seems happier this year," Jill said. "I can understand why. Entertaining the parade's special guests sure beats handling all the problems I've had to cope with."

Aileen wagged a finger at Jill. "Oh, come on. You know that heading the parade means that the higher-ups have confidence in you. If it goes off well, you'll be in a good position to become the vice president of public relations."

"Do you think it's possible that Neil is resentful that you got the job and he's trying to make things difficult?" Nancy asked, thinking out loud.

Jill shook her head. "Neil's been nothing but a help. I couldn't have gotten through the explosion without him," she said.

Just then one of the guards knocked at the door and told Aileen that her crew was ready to leave. As the reporter said goodbye and left the office, Nancy looked at her watch.

"It's almost nine o'clock," she told Jill. "Are you going to the party at Morelli's? I'm supposed to meet Bess there."

Jill got to her feet and let out a deep sigh. "I'm not in much of a party mood, but I guess the head of the parade should put in an appearance," she said. "Let's go."

Morelli's was an Italian bistro with an espresso bar and several tables arranged around a large dance floor. The iron-backed chairs reminded Nancy of the outdoor cafés in Europe. Waiters in short, tight-fitting red jackets glided among the maze of tables holding trays of delicious-looking food over their heads. Red lights shone down on the crowded dance floor, and rock music vibrated through the room. A curved staircase rose up to a balcony overlooking the dance floor.

Nancy spotted Bess at a large, crowded table near the staircase, talking to Greg. "Nancy! Jill!" Bess shouted, waving at them. "I thought you'd never get here!"

Nancy slipped into an empty seat at the table

as Jill went over to talk to Neil, who was standing by the stairs.

"These are some of the other parade guests," Greg told her, gesturing to the people seated at the table. He introduced the model Lauren Brown, Marshall Garton, the Olympic skier, and Pam Hart, the actress.

Nancy couldn't help being awed. Turning to Pam, who was sitting closest to her, Nancy said, "I loved your last movie."

"Thanks," Pam replied, smiling. "I'm working on the sequel now."

"Oh, Nancy, look what I bought at Mitchell's before we came here." Bess tapped a multicolored silk scarf that was knotted around her neck. "Neil and Greg insisted that I splurge."

"It's beautiful," Nancy told her. She looked up as Neil and Jill joined them.

"Okay, everyone, it's time to boogie!" Neil said. He grabbed Nancy's hand and led her to the dance floor.

Before Nancy knew it, everyone from the table was moving to the music. She smiled as she saw Greg twirl Bess around. Obviously Bess's thoughts were on romance, not mystery, tonight. Even Jill seemed to be having a good time. Nancy relaxed and let the music take over, pushing all thoughts of the explosion and break-in from her mind.

* * *

"I don't know, Nancy. It sounds dangerous," Eloise Drew said the next morning. She and Nancy were cleaning up the breakfast dishes in the small kitchen of her apartment in Greenwich Village.

Nancy had just filled her aunt in on her plan to go talk to Louis Clark. She was struck by how much her aunt looked like her father, Carson Drew. They had the same lustrous brown hair and elegant features. But at the moment, her aunt's forehead was wrinkled with worry lines.

"I have to start somewhere. It's already Tuesday, and Louis Clark is my only suspect right now," Nancy explained.

"Can't you just enjoy Thanksgiving without all of this detective stuff?" Eloise asked. Then she chuckled and added, "Of course you can't. You're Nancy Drew."

She smiled and kissed Nancy on the cheek. "What should I tell Bess when she wakes up?"

Nancy started for the hall closet to get her coat. "I'll probably be back before then!"

Nancy took a taxi to Clark's Department Store, which was located just a few blocks south of Mitchell's on Broadway. She stopped at the information desk on the ground floor and learned that Louis Clark's office was on the seventh floor, so Nancy took the escalator.

Unlike Mitchell's offices, Clark's were on the same floor as one of the selling areas. They were set apart only by a hallway stretching back from the housewares department. At the end of the hall was an open area with a reception desk. A gray-haired woman sat at the desk.

"Can I help you?" she said.

Nancy took a deep breath. She hoped the story she had thought up would be enough to get her an interview with Louis Clark. She had worn a nice pair of tan pants and a blue blazer so she would appear more professional.

"Hi. I'm from *The New York Times,*" she fibbed, mentally crossing her fingers. "I know I should have called first, but I was passing by and thought I'd take a chance that he'd be in. I'd like to interview him for a feature we're doing on leading figures in New York commerce."

The woman gave Nancy an appraising look, then buzzed Mr. Clark's office. She spoke into the phone briefly, then hung up and turned to Nancy again.

"Mr. Clark has a meeting, but he can spare a few minutes for you. I'll take you back. His secretary is out sick." The receptionist ushered Nancy into a big office. A short, balding man sat behind a wide mahogany desk, chomping on a cigar. Nancy did a double take when she saw what was sticking out of his breast pocket. It was a white handkerchief with the letters L.C. embroidered on it!

"Thank you for seeing me on such short notice," Nancy began, sitting in one of the two upholstered chairs in front of the desk.

Louis smiled at her. "Always glad to oblige the press," he said.

And get publicity for your store, Nancy added silently. She started by asking a few simple questions, and soon Louis Clark was telling her the story of how his grandfather founded the store and built it up to be the best in New York.

While he spoke, Nancy glanced surreptitiously around his office. She didn't see anything that could link him to either the break-in or the explosion at Mitchell's Brooklyn warehouse—not that she would expect him to leave evidence lying in plain sight. She decided to try and goad him into making a slip.

"And is Clark's still number one?" she asked, pretending to take notes. "I've heard some people say that the Thanksgiving Day parade gives Mitchell's an advantage."

Louis Clark's face turned bright red at the mention of his competition. "I don't think so," he said, looking at her suspiciously. "Why are you asking this?"

"I'm just trying to get a sense of how you deal with your competition, Mr. Clark," Nancy told him.

"How— Why, you—" Louis pushed his chair back and stood up abruptly. "Get out!" he shouted angrily. "I don't know who you think you are, but if I ever see you around my store again, I'll ruin you *and* the Mitchell's Thanksgiving Day parade!"

Chapter

Five

Nancy stared blankly at Louis Clark. I sure found his sore spot, she thought.

Nancy quickly stood, mumbled an apology, and left the office. She was deep in thought as she rode the escalator down to the main floor. It was obvious that Louis Clark considered the Mitchell's Thanksgiving parade a huge thorn in his side. The question was, would he really make good on his threat to ruin it?

She still needed solid proof that he was behind the break-in and sabotage, but the handkerchief was a good start. She would have to find a way to make a more complete search of his office.

Nancy stepped outside onto the noisy street and walked to the subway entrance nearby. She bought a token and consulted the subway map to see which train would take her closest to her aunt's apartment. The downtown train she got on was crowded. The bright orange seats were all taken, but Nancy didn't mind standing. There were so many different people to look at—from teenagers with hair dyed purple and blue to businessmen with briefcases—that the ride passed quickly.

Before she knew it, she had reached her stop in Greenwich Village and was being swept upstairs to the street in the flow of people. A few minutes later, she was back at her aunt's.

"Nancy, I went out for a walk, and I saw the cutest shirt. You have to see it," Bess said as Nancy walked into the living room. Bess was sitting on the couch, sipping a glass of juice. She was wearing a black jeans skirt with a red sweater tucked into it, red wool tights, and short black boots.

"Did you have any luck at Louis Clark's office?" Eloise called from the kitchen. Normally she would have been at work, but because of Bess and Nancy's visit, she had taken off the three days before Thanksgiving.

"I may have found who's been trying to wreck the parade," Nancy announced, sitting down on the couch next to Bess.

Bess sat up straight. "Who?"

The night before, Nancy had told Bess about the break-in at the warehouse. Now she related what had happened during the fake interview she had conducted that morning. When she was done, Bess let out a sigh of relief.

"Nancy, thank goodness! I mean, I've been trying to have a good time, but I was scared I was going to go to jail."

"We still need hard evidence," Nancy cautioned.

"I'm sure we'll find it," Bess said, taking a sip of her juice. "Oh—by the way, Greg called. He and Neil are going to be sightseeing this morning, but they want to meet us for lunch at a place called Kim and Karen's Grill. He gave me the address."

Nancy raised an eyebrow at her friend. "Things seem to be getting serious between you and Greg."

Bess's face lit up at the mention of the actor's name. "He's great, Nancy," she said. "I mean, I don't think there's a chance for a major romance or anything, but I just like being with him."

"Well, before we go meet them for lunch, let's go see that shirt!"

Nancy and Bess were loaded down with bags when they arrived at the restaurant located in SoHo, an area of Manhattan known for its art galleries. They had spent almost two hours shopping in the unusual boutiques in Greenwich Village.

"I think that silk shirt I got will look great with

my new pants," Bess said as they entered the restaurant.

"Definitely," Nancy agreed. She spotted Greg and Neil waiting in a booth toward the back.

"Hi!" Bess said brightly as the two girls slid into the booth.

The two guys barely said hello. Nancy noticed that Greg wouldn't look Bess in the eye. What was going on? Why were they being so unfriendly?

"I'm starved," Nancy said, trying to break through the tension.

"Mmm," Greg said noncommittally. He stared down at his menu.

Bess shot Nancy an uncomfortable look as an uneasy silence settled over the table. It wasn't broken until the waiter came to take their order. Nancy and Bess ordered grilled chicken sandwiches on Italian bread, while Neil and Greg ordered hamburgers.

As Neil handed the waiter his menu, he turned to Bess. "So, have you cleared up your problem with the police?" he asked curtly.

"Neil told me you're the lead suspect in the explosion, Bess," Greg added, leveling a cool gaze at Bess.

Bess looked as if she was going to burst into tears. "It—it was all a misunderstanding!" she said. She got up abruptly and hurried to the bathroom at the rear of the restaurant.

Mumbling an excuse to the guys, Nancy quickly followed. When she entered the rest room, Bess was standing at the sink, wiping her eyes with a wadded-up tissue.

"Greg hates me," she said.

"He doesn't hate you," Nancy assured her. "He's just concerned. Don't worry, Bess. We're going to clear your name."

She felt terrible for Bess. It didn't seem fair for the guys to judge her when there wasn't any conclusive evidence.

The girls stayed in the rest room a few more minutes, until Bess's eyes became less bloodshot.

"Where's Greg?" Bess asked when they returned to their table.

"He's filming a talk show this afternoon, so he had to eat and run," Neil replied, nodding toward Greg's empty plate.

During the rest of the meal, Nancy tried to keep up the conversation while Bess silently picked at her grilled chicken sandwich.

"It must be fun entertaining so many celebrities," she said to Neil.

Neil shrugged. "It's a lot of work. I have to make sure they all get special treatment at their hotels and that they see the sights in New York. The good part is that everyone loves being in the parade, so they're all pretty friendly. Take Greg —who would ever guess that someone so famous and good-looking would be so down to earth?"

Nancy felt Bess shift uncomfortably in her seat.

"He looks just like his pictures," Nancy said, trying to keep the conversation going. "I don't think he could take a bad photo. I bet even the photo on his driver's license looks good."

Neil laughed and pulled his wallet from his back pocket. "I take horrible pictures. Look at this." He pulled out his Mitchell's Department Store ID card. "I look like I'm sneezing."

"Your face *does* look a little twisted," Nancy said, smiling. She showed the ID to Bess, but Bess merely nodded. After they talked a little longer, Neil excused himself, saying he had to get back to the store. "The man who's playing Santa is coming for a rehearsal. Jill's swamped, so I said I'd handle it.

"Oh—by the way, I've organized a party tonight at the dance club Inverted," he added. "We'll be there around nine o'clock." He wrote down the address for the girls, paid the bill, and then rushed out the door.

It wasn't until after he was gone that Nancy noticed his Mitchell's ID lying on the table. "Oh, no—he forgot this." She picked up the card and slipped it into her bag. "I guess I'll give it to him at the club later."

Bess didn't seem to have heard. She was staring down at her plate in silence. After a long pause, she finally spoke.

"Thanksgiving is ruined," she said. "Greg hates me. He just left without even saying goodbye."

Nancy wasn't sure what to say. Greg *had* acted very coolly toward Bess. "Well, if he's going to be so quick to judge you, that says a lot about the kind of guy he is. I don't think you should let him ruin your vacation."

"You're right," Bess said, giving Nancy a weak smile. "This *is* Thanksgiving. It would just be more fun if Greg weren't mad at me, that's all."

Nancy smiled and said, "Come on. Jill invited us for a behind-the-scenes look at the parade. Let's go over to Mitchell's and see what's happening this afternoon. Maybe we'll even see Santa rehearsing!"

"What do you mean the clown costumes haven't arrived yet?" Jill was saying into her telephone receiver as Nancy and Bess arrived at her office.

Seeing Nancy and Bess, Jill waved them in. A moment later she hung up the phone and smiled at the girls.

"How would you two like to take a walk with me?" she asked. "One of the two companies that are providing our clown costumes keeps delaying delivery. My assistants haven't had any luck getting them, so I've got to go myself."

"Sure, we'll come along," Bess said.

As they made their way down to the street, Nancy noticed that Jill seemed more relaxed than she had since Nancy and Bess's arrival. "How's everything going?" Nancy asked.

57

"Actually, today is the first day in a while that I feel in control," Jill explained. "Neil let me know that the celebrity guests have been arriving on time, and the guest who was sick called to say she'll be able to make it, after all. She'll arrive Wednesday night. Except for these clown costumes, everything seems to be falling into place."

Jill told the girls that the costume store was about ten short blocks from Mitchell's in the theater district, and she suggested they walk. "This is a great city to walk in," Jill said. "It's the best way to see it—and sometimes the quickest way to get around." As they walked, they passed theater marquees advertising various plays. The costume store was located near a large theater. A black sign above the door read Disguise, Inc. Three mannequins were in the window, dressed as a fairy princess, a mermaid, and a soldier.

A bell rang as they entered the shop. A glass case with a cash register at one end ran along one wall. Racks filled with costumes and tables loaded with props and hats were squeezed into the rest of the space.

"Hello. May I help you?" asked a short, gray-haired man who stood behind the glass counter.

"I'm here to pick up the clown costumes for the Mitchell's parade," Jill said.

The man gazed at Jill uncomprehendingly. "They were delivered to the store yesterday."

"They were supposed to be, but my staff never received them," Jill said firmly.

"No, miss, I am sure they went out yesterday," the gray-haired man said. He shuffled back behind the counter and picked up a pile of receipts. "Let's see. The records of yesterday's deliveries are right here," he murmured, flipping through the stack. "Lane, Lansman, Marshall, ahh— Mitchell's." He held up the pink paper. "Here's the receipt."

Jill frowned. "That's impossible," she said. "Who signed for the costumes?"

Nancy and Bess gazed over Jill's shoulder at the pink slip on the counter. All three of them gasped as they read the signature.

There, next to the *X,* was the name Bess Marvin.

Chapter

Six

I—I COULDN'T have signed for them!" Bess stammered, turning red. "I've never even seen any clown costumes!"

Jill took a deep breath. "Bess, are you *sure* you didn't sign for the delivery?" she asked in a tight voice. Nancy could tell she was trying hard to control her anger.

"Bess doesn't even work for the store. She *wouldn't* have signed for them," Nancy said before Bess could answer. "Plus, we were in your office together. If anyone had asked her to sign for something, I would have seen it." First the explosion, and now this, she thought. Something about the whole thing smelled like a setup.

"Nancy's right," Bess said, giving Nancy a grateful look for coming to her defense.

Had someone tricked Bess into signing for the

costumes? Nancy wondered. Or had they forged her name? "Bess, let's compare your signature with the one on the receipt," she suggested.

Jill asked the man behind the counter for a pen and a piece of paper, and Bess wrote out her full name. The signatures matched exactly.

"Well, that's just great," Jill muttered angrily. Turning away from Bess, she stormed to the other side of the shop. "I don't care who signed for them, I still need those costumes!" she said.

"They were delivered to you," the shopkeeper shot back, following her. "Either you return them, or you pay me for them!"

While the two argued, Nancy turned back to Bess. "Someone may have tricked you into signing that receipt," Nancy said in a low voice. "Think hard, Bess. Have you signed *anything* since we've been in New York?"

Bess closed her eyes, her brow furrowed in concentration. "The only thing I've signed was the charge receipt for the scarf I bought at Mitchell's yesterday evening when I was with Neil and Greg, on our way over to Morelli's," she said.

"Are you sure you signed a charge receipt and not something else?" Nancy asked.

Bess bit her lip. "We were in such a hurry, and I was talking to Greg. I just signed what was put in front of me," she said. "I guess it could have been anything."

"Such as the delivery receipt for the costumes," Nancy suggested. She tried to think of who could have set up Bess. Louis Clark, her only suspect for the explosion and break-in, would hardly have been able to pull off the ruse without being noticed. Plus, he didn't even know Bess. On the other hand, maybe he was working with a Mitchell's employee who had seen Bess at the warehouse or the offices.

"Look, why don't you two go sightseeing this afternoon," Jill said, breaking into Nancy's thoughts. "I have to go make sure the costumes aren't anywhere in the store. Then I have to call around to see if someone—anyone—can deliver new costumes to us overnight." Before Nancy could offer to help, Jill stormed out of the shop.

"It's not too late to fly home and celebrate Thanksgiving in River Heights," Bess said, staring after Jill's retreating form. "Of course, now that I'm a wanted criminal, I can't even leave the state."

Nancy put a comforting arm around Bess's shoulder. "Don't worry, we'll get to the bottom of this," she said. "We have to do all we can to find out who set you up."

"We could talk to the salespeople at Mitchell's scarf counter," Bess suggested, her expression brightening. "I wish I had the receipt, but I think it's at your aunt's."

"Well, we're meeting Aunt Eloise for tea later, right? I'll call her and ask her to bring the charge receipt. And I'd like to talk to the person from here who delivered the costumes," Nancy added. "Maybe he or she can describe the person who really accepted the delivery."

"Which salesperson helped you that night?" Nancy asked as she and Bess paused at the edge of the U-shaped scarf counter at Mitchell's Department Store.

Bess stared at the two women who were waiting on customers. "I don't remember," she said glumly. "It could have been anyone."

Nancy hoped they would have more luck here than they had had talking to the delivery boy from Disguise, Inc. He had returned to the store while the girls were there, but he hadn't been able to offer much information. There had been so many deliveries the day before that he couldn't even remember whether a man or a woman had signed for the costumes at Mitchell's. He didn't have any idea what the person looked like.

"Can I help you?" An elegantly dressed woman came over to Nancy and Bess.

"My friend here bought a scarf last night," Nancy said. "I was wondering if we could talk to the salespeople who were working then or see your record of the purchase."

The young woman looked curiously at Bess. "I was working last night," she said. "The other salesperson, Diana, who was working with me has the day off. Was it cash or charge?"

"Charge," Bess answered.

"I'll be right back," the saleswoman said, leaving the counter and heading toward the back of the store. She returned a few minutes later with a metal file box. "What's the name?" she inquired.

Bess told her, and the woman quickly flipped through the file. "Here we are, one silk scarf," she announced, pulling out a yellow paper. "Is there a problem?"

"We just wanted to make sure it was signed," Nancy said vaguely. She was disappointed to see that Bess's signature appeared in the right spot.

"You should have been given the top copy of this, which has your original signature on it," the saleswoman went on to explain. "The sheet we keep is a carbon copy. Everything looks okay, except— Hmm, that's strange."

"What?" Bess asked, leaning forward.

The woman pointed to a box on the receipt labeled Sales Clerk. It was blank. "No one initialed this, which means that whoever rang up the sale won't get a commission. I can't imagine that either Diana or I would forget to fill that in. We were awfully busy last night, but still . . ."

But someone who wanted to set Bess up wouldn't have initialed it, Nancy thought. After thanking the saleswoman for her help, Nancy started to leave the area. Bess lingered behind, a sober expression on her face.

"What is it, Bess?" Nancy asked.

Bess blinked, then looked at Nancy. "I was just

thinking about Jules. Do you think he saw something before he was hurt in the explosion?" she asked. "I mean, maybe he's feeling well enough today to talk to us."

"Great idea, Bess!" Nancy said. "Let's find out!"

"Wow, this building is beautiful," Bess said a short while later, staring up at a building with an impressive carved stone facade.

Bonnie, Jill's assistant, had told the girls that Jules had been released from the hospital that morning and was recuperating at his family's apartment. When Nancy called him there, he readily agreed to talk to them. They immediately hopped into a taxi, which had just let them off in front of his building on Riverside Drive, on the Upper West Side. Across the drive a park stretched along the Hudson River. Nancy could see the George Washington Bridge in the distance, stretching across the river to New Jersey. A cold wind whipped up from the river, causing Nancy to pull her coat more tightly around her.

She and Bess hurried into the lobby and gave the uniformed doorman their names, saying that they were there to visit Jules Langley. After announcing the two visitors over the intercom, he directed them to the penthouse. When the girls stepped out of the elevator on the top floor, Jules was waiting in the open doorway.

"Hi, Nancy, Bess," he greeted them with a smile. "Come on in." His arm was in a sling, and there were some scratches and a dark bruise on his forehead. Still, he seemed to be in good spirits.

He led them through a spacious entry hall and on the living room, which was filled with antique furniture, a large oriental rug, and oil paintings. A large picture window provided a spectacular view of the Hudson River.

"How are you, Jules?" Nancy asked, sitting in a high-backed chair, while Jules and Bess settled on the couch.

"I'm a little bruised but basically okay," he replied. "Jill told me that the explosion was sabotage," he added, frowning. "Is that what you wanted to talk about?"

"Yes," Nancy said. "We're trying to find out who's responsible. Did you see anything unusual before the blast?"

"Not that I remember," he replied. "After I dropped you two at Jill's office, I went to the parade studio and watched them unwrap a few more balloons. The next thing I knew, I woke up in the hospital."

A look of disappointment crossed Bess's face. "Is there anyone you can think of who might be trying to sabotage the parade?" Bess asked Jules.

Jules looked down, and the color drained from his face.

"Jules, what is it?" Nancy asked. "If you know

something about the sabotage, you've got to tell us. It could save the parade."

He hesitated a moment before speaking. "My father is a . . . difficult man," he began. "When he first bought the store, over a year ago, he actually fired my two brothers—his own sons— when they voted against him in a board meeting."

Nancy couldn't imagine her own father doing something like that. It sounded to her as though Howard Langley was more than just difficult.

Jules raked a hand through his curly blond hair. "Dad didn't want to have the Thanksgiving Day parade. It costs so much money, and the store isn't doing very well," he went on. "About eight months ago, when we were launching our new cosmetics line, I made a deal with him. Dad agreed that if the new cosmetics brought in enough money, we'd go ahead with the parade."

"The line was a success, right?" Bess guessed.

"Right," Jules answered proudly. "Dad gave the go-ahead for the parade. But now we're launching our signature perfume and cologne, and we've spent hundreds of thousands of dollars in advertising and sample costs. Plus we've been laying out money left and right for the parade. Basically, we've drained the store's cash reserves, and my father's not happy, to say the least."

Nancy and Bess exchanged a silent look as Jules paused and shifted on the couch.

"We're committed to having the parade this

year, but next year is a different story," Jules continued. He looked straight at Nancy, a troubled look in his eyes.

"I think my father is trying to ruin the Thanksgiving parade so that no one will ever want to have it again!"

Chapter

Seven

WHAT!" BESS EXCLAIMED. She looked at Jules as if he had lost his mind. "Do you really think he would wreck his own store's parade?"

Jules let out a long breath. "Maybe I'm wrong—I hope I am. But I know how strongly my father opposes the parade. And with all the store's money troubles . . ."

Nancy was as surprised as Bess. "What about the explosion?" she asked Jules. "People were hurt."

"Including me." Jules shook his head ruefully. "Dad had no way of knowing I would be there when it went off. In fact, I'm convinced that the timer was set incorrectly. My father probably meant for it to go off at night, when no one was there. He would never hurt anyone intentionally," he said firmly.

There was a strange logic to Jules's explanation, Nancy realized. But there were still so many unanswered questions. Briefly she explained to Jules that she was a private detective, then said, "Jules, I'd like to talk to your father. That might help me get to the bottom of this."

After a long pause, Jules said, "Okay. But please, Dad can't know I told you any of this. I'll call and tell him you're a friend of mine who's interested in the retail industry. Otherwise, you'll have a hard time getting in to see him."

Nancy thanked him, and she and Bess stood up to leave.

It was almost four o'clock by the time the girls got off the subway near Mitchell's. Bess hesitated outside the revolving doors leading into the store.

"I think I'll go to Jill's office and try to help locate the missing costumes," she said. "I know she thinks I'm the leading suspect, but maybe helping out will prove to her that I wasn't responsible for any of the sabotage. I want her to know that I have nothing to hide."

Nancy gave her friend an encouraging smile. "That sounds like a good idea. I'll meet you in Jill's office after I talk to Mr. Langley."

"Ms. Drew?"

Nancy looked up from the newsmagazine she had been flipping through in the ninth floor reception area outside Howard Langley's office. "Yes?"

"Mr. Langley will see you now," said the receptionist, a tall woman with short salt-and-pepper hair.

Nancy put down the magazine and followed the woman down a hall, through two wooden doors, and into a huge office with windows along two walls. A gray-haired man in his sixties stood up from behind a long mahogany desk. He had the same blue eyes and athletic frame as Jules, Nancy noticed. Mr. Langley was much more conservatively dressed, however, in a charcoal gray suit and striped tie.

"Hello, Nancy," Mr. Langley greeted her. "I understand you have an interest in the retail industry."

"Yes," she replied, taking a seat in one of the leather chairs in front of his desk. "I'm especially interested in the Thanksgiving parade. I've been talking to Jill Johnston, and—"

"I don't want to talk about that parade," Mr. Langley interrupted, frowning.

Nancy could tell she had hit a nerve. "But it's really the thing that sets Mitchell's apart from your competition, don't you think?" she pressed.

Sitting behind the large desk, Mr. Langley shot her a stern gaze. "The vultures are waiting for me to collapse so they can come in and start picking apart my empire. Because of this parade, they just might get what they want." He let out a bitter laugh. "Since you spoke to Jill Johnston, you might already know that someone is apparently trying to sabotage the parade. If you ask me, whoever's behind it is doing Mitchell's a favor. Now maybe the other board members will realize what a mistake the parade is to begin with!"

Nancy could hardly believe her ears. Everything Howard Langley was saying backed up Jules's theory. She still didn't know how Louis Clark's handkerchief fit into the sabotage, but perhaps Mr. Langley could provide some clue.

"Do you think it's possible that Louis Clark is behind the sabotage?" Nancy asked.

"I doubt it," Mr. Langley said without hesitation. "That's a little drastic, even for Louis."

But was it too drastic for Mr. Langley himself? Nancy decided to try and shock him into revealing something about the sabotage. "Some people think that the person trying to sabotage the parade works here in the store," she said slowly. "It might even be someone in upper management. Would you agree with that?"

Mr. Langley's expression darkened, and he looked sharply at Nancy. "I don't know what you're trying to prove, young lady, but I think it's time for you to leave." He got up from behind his desk, went to the door, and opened it.

Great, now you've completely alienated him, Nancy chastised herself. It was too late to take back what she had said, however, so she simply thanked him for his time and left.

As she rode the elevator down to the eighth floor, where Jill's office was, Nancy thought over the case. Mr. Langley could easily have arranged the explosion. He also had the resources to have one of his employees sign for the costumes, hide them, and then set up Bess. No one would suspect that the owner of Mitchell's would ruin his own store's parade. But what Nancy still didn't understand was, why frame Bess?

When Nancy got to the open area outside Jill's office, she saw that it was a madhouse. People were scouring phone books and making calls to try to locate new clown costumes. Through the open door to Jill's office, Nancy saw Bess sitting alone, in the chair next to the desk.

Nancy hurried in and told her friend what had happened with Howard Langley. Bess stared glumly down at the desk while Nancy spoke. She barely seemed to be listening.

"The police were here before," Bess said when Nancy was done. "Jill called them about the costumes. I know they didn't believe my explanation about being fooled when I signed for the scarf. They even called Greg and Neil to verify that they were with me. And Jill still doesn't trust me," she went on quietly. "She's barely talking to me. Nancy, they haven't found enough replacement clown costumes yet—"

Bess stopped talking as Jill walked in and sat at her desk. Jill nodded to Nancy but didn't acknowledge Bess.

"Bonnie and I checked everywhere in the store we could think of for the costumes, without any luck. Some of the clowns are just going to have to devise their own costumes, that's all," Jill said with a sigh. "We're lucky that Disguise, Inc. was only providing about half the clown costumes. The other distributor's costumes have been here since Monday. So at least we have *them.*"

From the way Jill kept avoiding Bess's gaze, it was obvious that she blamed Bess for the lost costumes. Nancy wanted to clear her friend, but she decided to hold off telling Jill about her suspicions of Mr. Langley. After all, he was Jill's boss and the owner of Mitchell's. Without solid proof, Nancy couldn't expect Jill to believe the theory that he was the saboteur.

"Is there anything we can do to help?" Nancy offered. "We're supposed to meet Aunt Eloise for tea, but we have a few more minutes."

"Go on ahead. I wish I could do the same," Jill said wearily.

The girls decided to walk the half-dozen blocks to the café where they were meeting Nancy's aunt. They had gone only a few blocks when Nancy grabbed Bess's arm.

"Hey, that's Jill's friend Aileen," Nancy said, pointing to the other side of the street. "She was at the warehouse yesterday, covering the parade for the TV station she works for."

A camera crew was assembled in front of a small brownstone building. On one side of it was a skyscraper and on the other side was a large empty lot. Aileen stood in front of the camera, speaking into a microphone.

"Let's see what she's reporting about," Bess said.

The two girls waited for the light to change, then crossed the avenue and joined the small crowd that had gathered. A small group of people walked in a circle, carrying signs protesting the demolition of the historic building, where a famous writer had lived. As Nancy and Bess listened to Aileen's report, they learned that the building was to be demolished Thanksgiving Day, and another skyscraper was scheduled to go up on the brownstone lot and the empty lots adjoining it.

"Yikes!" Nancy whispered, glancing at her watch. "We're already fifteen minutes late meeting Aunt Eloise!"

They didn't want to disrupt Aileen's report, so they moved quietly away and hurried the last few blocks to the café. Eloise was waiting at a table by the window. She waved when she saw them approaching.

"Mmm, it smells great in here," Bess said as she and Nancy sat down. The aromas of fresh coffee and baked goods wafted through the tiny café, and a delicious-looking array of pastries and cakes was arranged in the glass counter against the wall.

Eloise's expectant gaze flitted back and forth between Nancy and Bess. "Okay, tell me everything," she said. "Why did you want me to bring Bess's sales receipt? I can feel it in my bones that something is going on."

Nancy and Bess quickly told Eloise all that had happened, stopping only to order three teas and some puffy pastries with whipped cream and chocolate. While Nancy's aunt listened, she reached into her purse and pulled out a white charge receipt. Nancy leaned forward to examine it.

"Bess, your signature is a carbon!" she said excitedly. Seeing Bess's confused expression, she explained, "The saleswoman said that your copy of the receipt should have your original signature on it, remember? Well, the salesperson's writing is original, but since your signature is a carbon copy, I bet that someone stuck something *else* on top of this and that's what you actually signed."

Bess's blue eyes widened. "That could have been the receipt for the costumes!" she exclaimed.

"So someone really *is* trying to set up Bess," Eloise said, taking a sip of her tea. "And from what you've told me so far, your suspects seem to be Louis Clark and Howard Langley."

Nancy frowned. "They're not exactly the easiest people to investigate." She sat up abruptly as a thought occurred to her. "Hey, don't most offices close at five o'clock?" she asked.

"Yeah," Bess replied. "So?"

"So, it's after five now. But most department stores stay open until at least six," Nancy said.

Eloise stared at Nancy. "You're not thinking what I think you're thinking—are you?"

Nancy exchanged a look with Bess, then said to her aunt, "I know you feel responsible for us, but clearing Bess is really important. If sneaking into Louis Clark's office gives us proof against him, then that's what I'm going to do."

After a short silence, Nancy's aunt threw up her hands. "Well, I can't let you two go alone. If you're going, so am I. Nancy, you always add excitement to my life when you come to visit," she said with a smile.

"Here goes," Nancy said under her breath some fifteen minutes later. She, Bess, and Eloise were pretending to browse through the housewares department on the seventh floor at Clark's. To their right was the hallway that led back to Louis Clark's office. Luckily, the salesman was helping another customer and had his back to them.

Signaling to Bess and her aunt, Nancy started casually down the hallway. She was relieved to see that the area near Louis Clark's office was deserted. The door was locked, but it was a simple lock, and Nancy was able to open it using a credit card. In a moment, the three were safely inside the office, with the door locked behind them.

"Look for anything unusual, or anything dealing with the parade or the explosion," Nancy whispered. "I doubt he would hide the costumes here, but maybe we'll find something indicating who his connection is at Mitchell's."

She started at Louis's desk, while Bess and Eloise looked through the shelves and closet. All the papers on the desktop seemed innocent enough—memos, marketing reports, and publicity strategies. After quickly flipping through them, Nancy started to open desk drawers. She came to a halt at the fourth drawer down.

"What's this?" she murmured. A small wooden rack of test tubes was nestled on top of some papers. Nancy took out the rack, then carefully uncapped one of the tubes and sniffed the fragrant, musky liquid inside. She recapped it and sniffed the liquid in another tube. It was similar to the first but slightly fruitier. When Nancy smelled the third test tube, she knew immediately that she had smelled the scent before.

"Bess, Aunt Eloise, come here!"

"What is it?" Bess asked as she and Nancy's aunt hurried over to the desk.

"Do you have the sample of Forever that Jules gave us?" Nancy asked Bess.

Bess rummaged through her bag and pulled out the small vial of perfume, which she handed to Nancy. Nancy pulled the top off and sniffed. Then she took another whiff of the liquid in the test tube.

"Nancy, what does this have to do with the parade?" her aunt asked, looking confused.

Nancy couldn't keep the excitement from her voice as she said, "I think Louis Clark is trying to steal Mitchell's exclusive perfume!"

Chapter

Eight

YOU'RE KIDDING!" Bess exclaimed. She sniffed the two fragrances. "They really do smell exactly the same," she agreed.

"Yes, but that doesn't seem like enough to prove that he stole Mitchell's scent," Eloise pointed out.

Her aunt had a point, Nancy realized. Looking back in the drawer, she saw a sheet of paper with several formulas written on it. Next to the formulas labeled #3, there was an asterisk and the word Forever, followed by a question mark.

"Here's our proof!" Nancy exclaimed. She pointed to the #3 label on the test tube she was holding, then showed Bess and her aunt the matching formula on the sheet.

"Plus Louis's handkerchief was found at the warehouse," Bess added excitedly. "That must be why he broke into the lab, to steal the formula!"

Nancy's aunt still didn't look convinced. "I think you should be sure before you go accusing the owner of one of the biggest department stores in New York. Why don't you ask Jules if this formula is an exact match of the formula for the perfume?

"Good idea," Nancy agreed. "We still don't know if Louis is connected to the sabotage, either."

While Bess and Eloise finished searching the office, Nancy tiptoed out to the reception area and made a copy of the formulas on the photocopy machine behind the receptionist's desk.

When Nancy returned, she could see that her aunt appeared nervous. "We've been here an awfully long time," Eloise said. "Shouldn't we—"

Her hand flew to her mouth as the doorknob to the office rattled. "Oh, my!" she whispered. A moment later they all heard the sound of a key being inserted in the lock.

"Hide!" Nancy whispered urgently.

Eloise and Bess dashed for the closet while Nancy ducked under the desk. Nancy's heart pounded in her chest as the door opened. Then a voice muttered, "Uh-oh, forgot the vacuum cleaner."

Nancy let out a sigh of relief as the door closed again and the person's footsteps receded down the hallway. "It was the cleaning lady," she whispered to Bess and her aunt. "Let's get out of here before she comes back." '

They quickly returned the test tubes and formulas to Louis Clark's desk drawer. Then, slipping the copy of the formulas in her pocket, Nancy led the way back out to the housewares department. A muffled announcement told them that Clark's was about to close, so the three blended in with the crowd exiting the store.

"My, that was a close one!" Nancy's aunt said once they were out on the street. "I don't know about you two, but all of this excitement has made me hungry again."

Bess pointed to Los Amigos restaurant down the street. "How about Mexican?" she suggested. "I want nachos, tacos, the works."

Nancy grinned at her friend. Bess was cheerful and hungry—she seemed to be back to her old self. Things were definitely looking up!

"It's too bad Eloise decided not to come to the club with us," Bess said as she and Nancy entered Inverted later that night.

"I guess the club scene just isn't for her," Nancy said, speaking loudly to be heard above the pulsing rock music. "Besides, she said herself that she was too exhausted by all our snooping around to do anything else tonight."

After dinner, Eloise had taken a cab back to her apartment, stopping first to drop off the girls

at Inverted, a club in a deserted warehouse area.
Now, after checking their coats, Nancy and Bess
paused to look around the club.

· There were pink plastic tables, and billowy
taffeta curtains covered the walls of the large
room. The place looked as if it had once been a
garage for a trucking company—several steel
garage doors remained, blending in with the
eclectic decor. A long bar stretched against one
wall, and the tables were scattered around the
dance floor. Platforms with more tables had been
constructed at various levels, with industrial
metal staircases leading up to them. Women
wearing glittering dresses and men in suits stood
side by side with teenagers with dyed hair and
leather jackets.

"Look, there's Dan," Bess said, pointing.

Nancy recognized Jill's dark-haired assistant.
He was up on one of the platforms, sitting with
Bonnie and several other people. Neil was also
there, talking to the actress Pam Hart. Nancy
didn't see Jill or Greg Willow, though.

The two girls made their way across the club
and up the stairs to the platform. At a distance
they saw Jules Langley and his father. Several
hellos sounded out, and Dan stood up and asked
Bess to dance with him. Nancy sat down next to
Neil.

"Hi. How's everything?" she asked.

"Busy." Neil ran his hand through his brown
hair. "Jill's still back in her office at the store.

There's some problem with police security for the parade."

It was difficult to hear him with the music blaring, so Nancy leaned closer. "Mmm, nice cologne," she commented.

"Thanks. You're getting a preview," Neil explained, grinning at her. "It's Forever Male, Mitchell's exclusive cologne. It goes on the market next month, along with the women's perfume. I'm one of the few people to be wearing it already."

"That's right. Jules mentioned a cologne when he gave us a tour of the cosmetics lab yesterday," Nancy said. "Oh—before I forget . . ." She reached into her bag and pulled out Neil's Mitchell's ID card. "You left this at Kim and Karen's Grill today."

Neil looked surprised as he took the card from her. "I was wondering where this went," he told her. "Thanks."

"How did you get along without it?" Nancy asked. "Don't you need it to get around the store?"

"I got a replacement," he replied, his gaze sweeping over the dance floor below. Nancy noticed him frown as he focused on something.

Looking down, she saw that Bess was talking to Greg Willow. He had an uncomfortable expression on his face, and he kept glancing nervously around the club.

"I really don't think our grand marshal should be involved with Bess," Neil said.

Nancy felt herself bristle. "If you're talking about the sabotage, Bess is *not* guilty," she insisted. "Can't you see that someone is setting her up—"

Her voice trailed off as she glanced down at the dance floor again. Greg was gesturing angrily at Bess now—it was obvious that he was yelling at her. For a moment Bess just stared at him, red-faced. Then she abruptly turned away and hurried toward the club's exit.

"Oh, no!" Nancy didn't even bother to say goodbye to the others. She grabbed her purse and raced down the stairs after Bess. She caught up with her at the coat check.

"Bess! What happened?" Nancy asked.

Tears were streaming down Bess's face. "Greg t-told me that he can't see m-me anymore because no one thinks the grand marshal of the parade should be seen with the lead sabotage suspect!"

"That's awful!" Nancy said. She grabbed their coats as they were handed over, tipped the woman, then hurried from the club with Bess. Within moments, they had hailed a cab, and Nancy gave the driver her aunt's address.

Nancy put her arm around Bess's shoulders. "I know it must be hard to have Greg treat you so terribly," Nancy said. "First thing tomorrow I'm going to call Jules and find out if the formula we found in Louis Clark's office really is for Forever. If it is, that's a good start to proving to everyone that you're innocent."

Bess nodded, but she still didn't look very hopeful. For the rest of the ride back to Eloise's apartment, she remained silent. Once Nancy let them in the front door with her key, Bess headed straight for the bedroom.

"You girls are home early," Eloise said, stepping out of her bedroom in her nightgown and robe. "Bess, Greg just called."

Bess's mouth dropped open in amazement. "He did?"

Eloise nodded. "He said he wants to meet you, alone, at the parade studio, so you can talk things over and clear everything up."

"The parade studio?" Nancy echoed, frowning. "But he was just at Inverted. That's nowhere near Brooklyn."

"I'm sure he said the parade studio," Eloise insisted. "It does seem rather strange, though."

Bess was already hurrying back toward the door. "Maybe it's not so strange," she said. "Maybe he thought of something that might lead to the real culprit," she said excitedly. "Yes, that *must* be it. I've got to get over there."

"Bess, wait! This could be dangerous," Nancy cautioned, but she could see her friend wasn't going to change her mind. "Well, I'm going to go with you, then. There's no way you're going to that warehouse all by yourself."

"Be careful, girls," Eloise said. "Nancy, your father would have my head if he knew I was letting you go. If you two aren't back here in an hour and a half, I'm calling the police."

Nancy kissed her aunt. "Don't worry, we'll be home before then."

"Bess, I think I should go inside with you," Nancy said, staring out the cab window at the entrance to the Mitchell's warehouse. The street was deserted, and she didn't see the guard or Greg anywhere.

"No, Nancy. Greg said he wanted to see me alone," Bess said firmly. "I'll be fine."

Nancy frowned. "I'll give you five minutes," she agreed reluctantly. "But then I'm coming in to check on you."

Bess agreed, then got out of the cab and hurried to the entrance. Nancy was surprised to see that she had no difficulty opening the door. Could Greg have left it propped open for her? But then, how had *he* gotten in? Had Neil lent him his Mitchell's ID? Had he talked the guard into letting him in?

The more Nancy thought about it, the more concerned she became. The guard didn't appear. After a few minutes, she couldn't stand waiting any longer. After instructing the taxi driver to wait for her, Nancy got out and hurried toward the warehouse entrance. She paused outside the door, cocking her head to one side.

In the distance she could make out the faint sounds of sirens. The high-pitched whine grew louder, and moments later two police cars were barreling down the street toward the warehouse, their lights flashing. A black sedan was right behind them.

Nancy froze with fear as all three cars screeched to a stop at the curb in front of her. Jill jumped out of the black car, spoke briefly to the four officers, then led them into the warehouse.

"Jill! What are you doing here?" Nancy asked.

"I could ask you the same thing, but I don't have time, Nancy," Jill said. She quickly led the officers through the door and down the long hallway to the parade studio.

Nancy followed, a feeling of dread welling up inside of her. "Jill, I think you should know—"

Before Nancy could say anything more, Jill opened the door to the studio, and she and the officers rushed in. Nancy gasped as she stepped in after them.

The parade studio was bathed in light. Bess was standing in the center of the warehouse, her eyes wide with terror.

Half a dozen balloons were laid out on the floor around her—slashed to pieces!

Chapter

Nine

"I KN-KNOW THIS l-looks bad," Bess stuttered. "When I got here, the b-balloons were already slashed. Honest!"

Nancy hurried over to Bess and put an arm around her friend. "We just arrived a few minutes ago," Nancy explained to Jill and the police, one of whom was the detective who had questioned Jill about the fire. "Bess got a message to meet Greg Willow here."

Detective Green crossed his arms over his chest and glanced around. "Well, I don't see him, do you? All I know is that once again we've got a problem with the parade, and once again Bess Marvin is in the middle of it." He took a notebook from his back pocket and flipped it open. "All right, why don't you tell me the whole story?"

While Bess told Detective Green what had happened, Nancy went over to Jill, who was examining the slashed balloons. Jill's face was a mask of anger. "Where's the guard?" she snapped, looking around the cavernous room. "Why didn't he stop this?"

"I was wondering the same thing," Nancy said. "He wasn't outside when Bess and I arrived. Listen, about Bess—"

"I can't even look at her anymore, Nancy," Jill cut in, lowering her voice. "I know you think she's innocent, but she's been connected to almost every attack on the parade. I'm sorry, but I just don't trust her."

The two of them turned as one of the officers called out urgently from a float on the other side of the studio, "Detective! Over here!"

Nancy and the others hurried over to the young officer. He was bending over a uniformed guard who was bound and gagged.

"Oh, no!" Bess exclaimed, her hands flying to her face. "Is he okay?"

The officer quickly untied the guard and removed his gag. The guard looked surprised to see so many people in the parade studio. "I'm okay, except for this nasty bump," he reported, gingerly rubbing the back of his head.

"I don't know how it happened, Ms. Johnston," the guard went on. "I came in to make my rounds, and someone beaned me on the head from behind. I don't know who it was or how he got in here." He glanced at his watch. "That was about fifteen minutes ago. When I woke up just now, I was tied up, and you all were here."

"We're just lucky whoever it was left the door open," Jill said, with a critical glance at Bess. "If the door is left open too long, it triggers an alarm in the police precinct. By chance, I was on my way over here to pick up some papers I needed, and I saw the police pulling up ahead of me. It was a lucky coincidence." She glared at Bess.

"Wait a minute. You don't seriously think Bess did this?" Nancy said defensively. "We weren't even *here* fifteen minutes ago. Can't you see? Someone else did all this, then arranged the phony message so that Bess would come down here. The door was open when we got here. Someone *wanted* Bess to get in so she would get caught. Call my aunt. She's the one who took the message."

Nancy looked beseechingly at Jill, but Jill's expression still remained stony. Detective Green didn't look convinced, either. He finished taking Bess's statement, while the other officers searched the parade studio.

"My men didn't find a knife or any other sharp object Ms. Marvin could have used to slash the balloons. There's no sign of forced entry, either," Detective Green reported to Jill twenty minutes later. "We did find a small piece of cardboard taped over the door so that the lock couldn't engage." He nodded at Bess. "Do you want to press charges for breaking and entering?"

Bess grabbed Nancy's arm, her eyes wide with fear. Jill hesitated a moment, frowning, before she answered. "That won't be necessary."

Nancy was relieved when the police finally told the two of them they could leave. The two girls hurried outside to their waiting taxi.

"Nancy, I could've gone to jail tonight!" Bess wailed. "Why is someone doing this to me?"

"More importantly, *who* is doing this to you?" Nancy said, giving Bess's arm a squeeze. "The real saboteur wants to make sure you get caught, instead of him or her. And I seriously doubt that that person is Greg Willow. Whoever called just used Greg's name."

Bess wiped at her eyes and looked at Nancy. "Louis Clark?" she suggested.

"Or his connection at Mitchell's," Nancy added. "A lot of people from the store were at Inverted. Anyone could have seen you with Greg and known there's something intense between you. After we left, they could have left the message for you and then gone to the parade studio and knocked out the guard and slashed the balloons."

Bess reached into her bag, took out a tissue, and blew her nose. "What about Howard Langley? He was at Inverted tonight, too."

Nancy let out a sigh. "Maybe, but we can't pin

the sabotage on him *or* Louis Clark without more concrete proof." Her next words were swallowed by a huge yawn. "What we need is a good night's sleep. Maybe in the morning something will come to us."

"There's Jules," Nancy said Wednesday morning as she and Bess entered a coffee shop near Mitchell's Department Store.

"I hope he can prove Louis Clark really *is* stealing Mitchell's exclusive scent," Bess said. "Then maybe Louis will admit to the other sabotage, too, and my Thanksgiving will be saved."

"With any luck, the real culprit will be in jail before the day is out," Nancy said.

"Hi!" Jules greeted them as the two girls slipped into the booth opposite him. After the three of them ordered coffee and doughnuts, he leaned over the table. "I couldn't believe it when you called this morning about Louis Clark. So did he really steal our perfume?"

"You're the one who can tell us the answer to that question," Nancy said.

She reached into her bag and pulled out the photocopy of the formulas she'd found in Louis's office. Jules had a file with him. He opened it and looked back and forth from the file to the sheet.

"Let me see," he said, his brow furrowed in concentration. "Number three—this is it!" he yelled.

"Are you sure?" Bess asked, taking a sip of her coffee.

Jules nodded his head adamantly. "Positive. It's an exact match to the formula for Forever." He pounded his fist on the table. "Somehow Louis Clark got his hot little hands on a sample of our perfume! That's about the only way to re-create the formula exactly."

"We think that's why he broke into the lab on Monday," Nancy said. "We found a handkerchief with his initials on it inside."

"I don't know," Jules said. "It's virtually impossible to determine the formula overnight, even with a sample. Maybe he actually found the formula in the file."

"Maybe," Nancy said. "I'm going over to Louis's office right now to confront him."

"Good idea," Jules agreed. "I'd go with you, but I've got a doctor's appointment." He gestured to the sling protecting his left arm. "Let's meet back here in an hour so you can fill me in."

"I'm sorry, girls, but you need an appointment," Louis Clark's secretary said firmly.

Nancy saw Bess's disappointed look, but she wasn't about to give up that easily. "I thought I *had* an appointment," Nancy lied, raising her voice. If she made a big enough stink, maybe that would work.

"Yes," Bess chimed in loudly. "It's very important that we see Mr. Clark *now.*"

"Well, you can't. I—"

Just then the door to Louis Clark's office opened, and Louis appeared. "What's going on out here?" he asked.

Nancy held up the photocopy of the perfume formulas. "Recognize these, Mr. Clark?"

Louis's eyes widened at the sight of the formulas. His gaze flitted nervously around the reception area. "I, er, think I can spare a few minutes for these young ladies," he told his secretary, gesturing for Nancy and Bess to enter his office.

As soon as he shut the door behind the girls, Nancy squarely faced the store owner. "Mr. Clark, I know you're trying to steal Mitchell's exclusive perfume formula. I also happen to know you're missing a handkerchief—the one with the initials L.C. It was found in Mitchell's cosmetics lab in Brooklyn."

Louis stared impassively at Nancy and Bess as he walked to his desk and sat down. His initial nervousness had disappeared. "The police have already called me. A Detective Green, I believe. Nice fellow. He asked me some standard questions, and I told him I didn't know what he was talking about. I'm an important member of New York's business community," he added smugly. "No one's going to believe I would stoop so low as to break into my competitor's warehouse."

"You don't expect us to believe that, do you?" Bess asked angrily.

Louis let out a little laugh. "Business is a funny

thing," he said. "Ideas are stolen every day. By the time they're released to the public, no one's sure whose idea it really was in the first place."

"What are you trying to say?" Nancy asked.

"What if I said Mitchell's had stolen *my* scent?" Louis said. "How would they prove me wrong? It's a very difficult area of the law, not to mention a very expensive one. Mitchell's would be better off financially to forget about the whole thing than to fight me in court and risk losing." He smiled broadly at Nancy and Bess. "A photocopy of some formulas isn't exactly concrete proof."

Nancy exchanged a quick look with Bess. Louis Clark was smooth, all right. His smug attitude told her that he *had* stolen the formula—he'd practically admitted it to them! But he seemed to think he couldn't be caught. And if he wasn't going to admit to stealing the perfume, Nancy was sure he wouldn't admit to any sabotage, either. It looked as if she and Bess were back at square one.

"He's got some nerve!" Jules exclaimed. As planned, he met Nancy and Bess again at the coffee shop. Over mugs of hot chocolate, the girls told him what had happened in Louis Clark's office.

Bess frowned and propped her chin in her hands. "He's a criminal who might never get caught, and I'm a totally innocent person who might go to jail," she said. "Isn't there something we can do?"

"We have to tell my father," Jules said firmly. "He'll get his lawyers on it right away."

Suddenly his expression changed, and he looked nervously from Bess to Nancy. "Not to change the subject or anything, but my dad told me about what happened when you saw him yesterday, Nancy," he said, fidgeting with his mug. "Did you find out anything about the sabotage?"

Nancy shook her head. "Nothing concrete," she replied. She hesitated, then said, "I know this is a lot to ask, since he's your father—but is there any way you can help me get into his office when he's not there, so I can look for clues that might link him to the sabotage?"

Jules didn't answer right away. For a moment, Nancy was afraid he'd say no. Then he took a deep breath and said, "He's out at a meeting this morning with some of his creditors. We can go over now and tell the receptionist that we need to see him and that we'll wait in his office. I do that a lot."

After finishing their cocoa, the three walked to Mitchell's and made their way up to Howard Langley's ninth-floor office. Nancy stood behind Jules, hoping the receptionist wouldn't recognize her from the day before. She smiled when she saw

Jules. When he explained that they wanted to wait for his father, she waved them into the office. She hardly glanced at Nancy and Bess.

"Great!" Bess said as soon as Jules closed the door behind them. "What do we do now, Nan?"

"Look for the same kinds of things we did in Louis Clark's office," Nancy whispered. "Anything to do with the parade, the explosion, the missing costumes, the slashed balloons, or anything unusual."

Nancy walked over to Mr. Langley's desk and started searching through a stack of papers and files there. Bess went over to a console against the right wall and began looking around the television set and video cassette recorder, while Jules looked on the shelves.

Nancy didn't find anything unusual on the desktop, so she opened the top drawer. Just as she was about to reach inside, a booming voice startled her.

"What in the world is going on in here?"

Chapter

Ten

NANCY LOOKED UP from behind the desk to see Howard Langley looming large in the doorway, his hands on his hips and an angry expression on his face. "What is going on in here?" he repeated.

Nancy slowly closed the desk drawer. She shot a worried glance at Jules and Bess, who both looked as shocked and surprised as she felt.

"Uh, hi, Dad," Jules said. "Nancy and Bess were helping me get to work on an important assignment." His voice was steady, but Nancy noticed that his face was white.

"What important assignment, and how does it at all involve me, my office, and my private papers?" Howard Langley walked across the room, leveling a disapproving gaze at Nancy, who moved away from the desk. "Hello, Ms.

Drew," he said curtly. His eyes drifted to Bess, and he added, "I don't believe I know your other friend."

Jules introduced Bess, then said, "Dad, I have some bad news—"

"Jules, I just met with our creditors. I don't need any more bad news today," Mr. Langley said wearily.

Jules walked over and stood face-to-face with his father. "Louis Clark has stolen the formula for our new Forever perfume."

"What!" Mr. Langley exclaimed. His tired expression was immediately replaced by a look of outrage.

Jules, Nancy, and Bess quickly told him about finding the formulas and confronting Louis Clark. "That's why we were going through things," Jules concluded. "We wanted to gather any papers we could to prove that Mitchell's lab invented the perfume first."

Nancy had to admit Jules sounded believable. She held her breath, waiting to see if Mr. Langley would buy the story.

"I always love a fight," Howard finally said. He pressed a button on the intercom. "Call the lawyers," he yelled into the machine. His eyes held a challenging gleam as he turned back to Jules, Nancy, and Bess.

"I'm going to make sure Louis Clark is put in jail for trespassing at the lab and for stealing the perfume formula," Mr. Langley said. "We have every paper to prove that we created that scent. Louis won't have enough time to create a paper trail that's half as convincing."

Nancy looked over at Bess, who breathed a sigh of relief. Nancy could see that it was easier to be on the same side as Mr. Langley than to work against him. She remembered how sure of himself Louis Clark had been earlier that day. Now she knew that taking on Howard Langley wasn't going to be half as easy as Louis Clark had predicted.

The intercom on Mr. Langley's desk buzzed, and the secretary announced that the store's attorneys were on the line. Howard motioned for Jules and the girls to leave his office so he could speak to the lawyers in private.

Jules led Nancy and Bess out. As they rode the elevator downstairs, they breathed a collective sigh of relief.

"I thought for sure we were goners," Jules said. "I can't believe none of us heard him coming."

"I know! You did a brilliant job of covering, Jules," Bess said, grinning at him.

"It was perfect," Nancy chimed in.

With a nervous smile, Jules said, "At least the whole Louis Clark mess took Dad's mind off why we were sneaking around his office." His voice dropped to a whisper as he added, "I'll go home right now and look around his office there. Maybe I'll find something that links him to the sabotage. Where can I call you if I do?"

Nancy gave him her aunt's phone number, and then they went downstairs. Nancy paused just before the revolving doors leading outside and checked her watch. It was almost one o'clock.

"Um, Nan?" Bess said, biting her lip. "Maybe we should go to the parade studio and see if we can help repair the balloons," she suggested. "They can probably use all the help they can get. After all, the parade is tomorrow."

Nancy hesitated. After last night, she was sure Jill wouldn't want Bess anywhere near the parade studio. Then again, Bess *was* innocent. If they went to help out, Nancy would also have a chance to look for more clues as to who the real saboteur was.

Smiling at Bess, Nancy said, "Good idea. Let's grab a sandwich at the deli across the street, and then we'll get a cab to the parade studio."

Nancy and Bess arrived at the parade studio in Brooklyn just as one of the workers was exiting.

"Good," Nancy said under her breath to Bess, as the young man held the door open for them. "We don't have to worry about getting in."

After thanking the young man, the girls made their way down the hall to the studio. When they opened the door, the first thing Nancy saw was a camera crew over by the balloons. Aileen Nash was interviewing Jill, who explained on-camera that the police thought a neighborhood prankster had broken in and slashed the balloons.

"At least she isn't accusing me on TV," Bess whispered glumly as she and Nancy approached the camera crew.

Dozens of people were working to repair the balloons, using needles and a soft, rubbery material. On the other side of the room, final touches were being applied to some floats.

As Nancy and Bess listened to the interview, Jill explained that the balloons and floats would be transported later that afternoon to the Museum of Natural History in Manhattan. That was the starting point of the parade. Final preparations at the museum would last through the night until the parade began in the morning.

A few minutes later Aileen and Jill wrapped up the report. While the camera crew packed up, Nancy and Bess walked over to the two women.

"Hi, Nancy," Aileen said, smiling. Nancy introduced Bess to the newscaster. Bess said hello to Jill, but Jill just frowned and turned away. After saying something to one of the workers who was repairing balloons, Jill headed back toward the hallway.

"I, uh, I guess I'll ask these workers if there's anything I can do," Bess said uneasily.

"I'll tell Jill what we found out," Nancy said, purposely being vague about Mr. Clark and Mr. Langley so that she wouldn't give any information away to the reporter. "I know we don't have proof yet, but Jill has to recognize that you're not the only suspect for the sabotage."

Aileen fell into step with Nancy as she headed toward the hallway leading to Jill's office. "I take it your friend is the one Jill has been so upset about lately," Aileen said.

"Bess didn't do anything," Nancy said firmly.

"Whatever you say," Aileen said, but her tone revealed her doubts. When they got to Jill's office, Aileen waved a goodbye to Jill through the open doorway, then continued down to the outside door.

Nancy was relieved that the newswoman didn't linger. She didn't want anyone else around when she told Jill about the perfume formula—and about her suspicions of Howard Langley.

Jill was on the phone when Nancy walked into the office. "Yes, please have the helium delivered directly to the Museum of Natural History," she said. After talking a few moments longer, Jill hung up.

It took only a few minutes for Nancy to bring Jill up to date on her discovery that Louis Clark was stealing Mitchell's new perfume.

"Wow," Jill said, looking surprised. "So that really *was* his handkerchief you found here the other night."

Nancy nodded. "I have a theory about who might be responsible for sabotaging the parade, too." After taking a deep breath, she told Jill of Jules's theory that his own father was trying to ruin the parade. "I know it sounds crazy, but maybe he's trying to make sure the store doesn't ever have to lay out money for the parade again," she finished.

Jill's mouth had dropped open during Nancy's explanation. Now she sat quietly, a thoughtful look on her face. "Mr. Langley *does* hate the parade," she finally said. Then she shook herself. "I'm sorry, Nancy, but we can't rule out Bess," she said firmly. "All the evidence points to her."

Nancy let out a breath of frustration. "I just wish there was a way to prove that someone has been setting her up. Someone had to have come to the parade studio right before up last night, she said. "If there was only a way to keep track of everyone who comes and goes . . ."

Suddenly Jill blinked and straightened up. "Wait a minute—maybe there *is* a way!" she said excitedly. "All the locks are hooked into a main computer bank back at the store. The ID numbers are screened whenever someone uses a card to enter one of the restricted areas. It's a long shot, but maybe we can get some kind of computer record of who's been here during the last few days."

Nancy's heart pounded with excitement as Jill reached for her phone and punched in a number. "Then we could see who was in the warehouse at the time of the different incidents," Nancy said, thinking out loud. "There hasn't been any sign of forced entry, except for the break-in at the cosmetics lab. And we know that was Louis Clark. Chances are, the other attacks were made by a Mitchell's employee."

Jill nodded. "The list wouldn't include people like you and Bess, who enter the building with someone else, but it might provide some clue— Oh, hello, Richard. Jill here," she said into the receiver. She spoke briefly to the head of security at Mitchell's, then hung up and turned back to Nancy.

"They can't isolate one area, but they can send over a printout of everyone who's entered all restricted areas of the store, as well as the outside doors of the warehouses during the past week," Jill explained. "We'll have to go through and highlight the warehouse entries."

"Great!" Nancy said excitedly.

An hour and a half later, Jill's desk at the warehouse was covered with printouts that the head of Mitchell's security had sent over. Jill, Nancy, and Bess were all bent over the desk, each examining a different section of the printout.

"What's the code for the parade studio warehouse again—zero-one—five?" Bess asked, scanning the columns of numbers and names on her printout.

"That's right," Jill confirmed, without looking up from her own list.

At first Jill had resisted Nancy's suggestion that Bess help them, but when she saw the thick pile of printouts that arrived from the store, Jill had relented. Nancy was relieved that Jill was finally warming up toward Bess—even if it was only a little.

Since Nancy and Bess weren't familiar with the names of employees, they asked Jill every time they came to an entry for the warehouse. So far, all of the people listed were regulars who worked at the warehouse.

"Who's Heath Nealon?" Bess asked.

Nancy shrugged. "Hey, here he is on my sheet, too. According to this, Heath Nealon was here last night, just before eleven o'clock."

"Hey, that's right before we came," Bess added. "I bet he's the guy who slashed the balloons and knocked out the guard!" She pointed down at her printout. "He was here on Monday morning, too—the day of the explosion."

Jill glanced up from her printout, a puzzled look on her face. "I've never even heard of Heath Nealon," she said. "And I know the names of everyone working on this parade. Let me call personnel and ask if they have any record of him."

When she hung up the phone a few moments later, she was frowning. "Heath Nealon is a stockboy at the store," Jill explained to Nancy and Bess. "I don't know why he'd be at the warehouse. He has nothing to do with the parade."

"Can you call him to find out?" Bess suggested.

Once again, Jill picked up the phone on her desk. First she called Heath Nealon, and then she spoke with his supervisor. Nancy couldn't tell much from Jill's side of the conversation. She and Bess waited anxiously until Jill finished.

"So?" Nancy asked, leaning forward.

"Heath Nealon said he's never been to the parade studio," Jill began.

"But my printout says he was here Monday morning," Bess protested. "Besides, his supervisor can't know what Heath does at night, after work is over."

Jill held up a hand. "Actually, Heath told me something very interesting." She paused, giving Nancy and Bess a meaningful look. "A few days ago, his ID card was stolen!"

Chapter

Eleven

N ANCY AND BESS exchanged looks of shock.

"Are you sure he didn't lose it?" Bess asked.

Jill nodded. "He told me he always keeps it in the same place, in the pocket of his jacket, which he hangs on a hook in the stockroom. When he got to the store on Monday morning, he reached into his pocket for his card, and it was gone."

"Why didn't he report that it was missing?" Nancy wanted to know.

"I asked him the same thing," Jill told the girls. "He said he thought he'd get into trouble. Apparently a friend of his in the stockroom has been letting him in every morning."

Nancy's mind was racing. "So whoever stole his ID card is the real culprit," she said.

"But how can we find out who that is?" Bess

asked. "We only have until tomorrow morning to find out. What if the person does something terrible and tries to pin it on me again?"

"I think you're in the clear now," Nancy said. "You've never even been in the stockrooms or met Heath Nealon, so there's no way you could know where to get his ID card."

Seeing that Jill's expression was still guarded, Nancy added, "It's possible that Howard Langley has an employee doing his dirty work for him. That person could have stolen Heath Nealon's ID card."

Jill sighed, then smiled at Bess. "And I supposed we still can't be sure Louis Clark isn't a saboteur as well as a thief," she added.

"I just can't wait until everyone believes I'm innocent," Bess said.

"Well, the good news is that everything's on schedule," Jill said, changing the subject. "The repairs to the balloons are almost finished, and all the floats and balloons are being transported to the Museum of Natural History. Neil is making sure all the guests, bands, and other groups are checked in at the parade site by six in the morning."

Bess's expression brightened as she said, "It must really be something to see the balloons and floats being readied at the museum tonight."

Jill nodded. "It's a major preparade event. Tons of tourists and people from the neighborhood come to watch."

Nancy looked up to see Neil Steem walk into Jill's office. Greg Willow and a woman with curly red hair and a camera around her neck were with him.

"Hi!" Neil said brightly. "We came out to get a couple of publicity shots of Greg on the lead float."

Bess was fidgeting with the hem of her striped sweater. After all that had happened, she was obviously uncomfortable being in the same room as Greg. Greg looked a little nervous himself. He glanced at Bess out of the corner of his eye from time to time, but he wouldn't look at her directly.

"Um, excuse me. I think I'll go help out with the balloons." Bess stood up abruptly and hurried from the office.

Jill stared after her, then turned to Nancy. "I know you think I've been hard on Bess, but I think it would be a good idea if she stays away from all the parade sites from now on," Jill said. "That way no one can suspect her of anything else that might happen."

"I agree," Neil said. "There have been too many coincidences to take any chances."

Nancy sat in silence. How was she supposed to tell her best friend that she wasn't wanted? Jill and Neil were putting her in an awkward position.

"I'll take her out tonight," Greg volunteered.

Nancy looked at the actor in surprise. Was this the same guy who had told Bess he couldn't see her anymore? Why was he suddenly changing his mind?

Greg must have seen the confusion on her face. He stepped forward and said, "Nancy, I really like Bess. It's just that I have an image to keep up. Sometimes it's hard to follow your heart when everyone else is telling you it's a bad idea."

Greg glanced at Jill and Neil. "I just can't believe Bess would do any of the things she's being blamed for," he went on. "This is probably the last night I can see her here, and I want us to leave as friends. So I'm not going to listen to anyone but myself tonight."

"Bess will be really glad to hear that," Nancy said, smiling warmly at Greg. Whatever else happened, Bess would know that he believed in her, and Nancy knew how much that meant to her friend.

Neil and Jill exchanged a long look. Finally, Neil said, "If you really feel that way, I have passes to the Dot Matrix dance club tonight. Just stop by my apartment on your way. It's eighty-eight East Eighty-eighth Street, number eight D."

"No need to write that down," Greg said with a laugh. "I'll just go to the building with all the eights on it." Turning to Nancy, he asked, "Do you want to come with us tonight?"

"No, thanks," she said. "I'm going to keep an eye on the final preparations at the museum. I figure it's the last chance anyone has to ruin the parade, so I want to be there. Maybe this time, we'll catch this criminal in the act."

"I really need a break." Jill's assistant Dan wiped his brow and joined Nancy on a bench in one of the huge rooms in the Museum of Natural History.

"I know what you mean," Nancy agreed, looking up from the thick computer printout that Jill had gotten from Mitchell's security. She had brought as much of the printout as she could carry in her shoulder bag and had taken a break from the preparations to study it. "This place has been a madhouse for hours. There's so much going on, both inside and outside, it's hard to believe that it's three in the morning."

Nancy had arrived at the museum around six, after spending the afternoon helping Bess shop for an outfit to wear on her date with Greg. For several hours the huge space had been filled with curious spectators and camera crews who had entered through large metal doors that opened to the outdoors. Jill had explained that these rooms were usually used to work on the skeletons of large dinosaurs that were part of the museum's collection. Now they were filled with people doing last-minute work on balloons and floats for the Mitchell's Thanksgiving Day Parade.

So far, Nancy had seen over twenty-five floats and nine large helium balloons. Some were outdoors on West Eighty-first Street and others were inside the museum. Bonnie, Dan, Jill, Neil, and the other workers were busy putting finishing touches on some floats and checking to see that the balloons were filling evenly with helium. Thick ropes attached the balloons to heavy sandbags so they wouldn't float away. Even Mr. Langley was there, looking on from the sidelines.

"Your dad is the only one around here who doesn't seem excited about tomorrow's parade," Nancy had commented to Jules, who was also helping out.

"I didn't find anything in his study at home that links him to the sabotage," Jules told her. Letting out a sigh, he added, "I never thought I'd ask a detective to keep an eye on my own father, but I think that's what you'd better do."

Nancy had wandered through the cavernous rooms and gone out to Eighty-first Street, carefully watching everything, but so far she hadn't seen any foul play. Now it was so late that most of the camera crews and tourists had left. Nancy didn't see Jill or Mr. Langley around, either. The security guards and about twenty employees were still hard at work, though.

"So what happens next?" Nancy asked Dan.

"Well, things will be sort of quiet until around five A.M.—that's when the organizers and volunteers are due to show up. The parade guests, bands, and all the other participants should begin to get here soon after," Dan explained.

Glancing around, Nancy said, "I haven't seen Jill recently. Do you know where she is?"

"She's back in her office at the store, supervising the staff," Dan told her. "They're getting the costumes ready to be trucked up here." He stood up and added, "Actually, I should head over there now to help out."

"See you," Nancy said. After he left, she looked around. For the first time she realized she was alone in the room. Workers were either outside or working on the floats in the adjoining room. The lighting seemed dimmer than before, and the balloons cast eerie shadows on the walls.

After stuffing the printout back in her bag, Nancy got up and glanced around the huge room. There were so many places for the saboteur to hide that there was no way she could keep an eye on all of them.

Nancy jumped as she heard a sound close behind her. She quickly spun around—then let out a breath of relief.

"Oh, Jules, it's you," she said, with a weak smile. "You scared me."

"Sorry," he said. "I just came over to find out if you've seen anything suspicious."

Nancy shook her head. "Not yet," she replied. She paused and looked up at the enormous cat balloon that had been damaged in the explosion at the parade studio. The missing paw had been repaired, and the seam was only barely visible.

"Despite all the attacks, it looks as though the

parade will go off smoothly," Nancy said. "I'm glad that—"

Nancy broke off as a sharp tearing noise caught her attention. Looking down, she saw that one of the ropes supporting the balloon had snapped.

"Jules, the rope!" she cried, pointing. She gasped when she saw the other rope. It had begun to unravel as well. In another moment, it would snap, and the balloon would float up out of reach!

"Try to hold it," Jules said urgently. "I'll get help." He took off toward the next room.

Nancy bent and reached for the rope that hadn't broken yet. Grabbing it above the tear, she pulled down.

As she looked down to examine the rope more closely, her eyes widened. The rope looked as if it had been cleanly cut halfway through.

"Someone deliberately cut it!" she said softly.

Nancy was about to yell for Jules when she was suddenly hit on the back of the head. The last thing she was aware of was a sweet scent drifting past her nostrils as the rope began to slip from her fingers.

Then there was blackness.

Chapter

Twelve

Nancy slowly opened her eyes, wishing she could make the dull, throbbing pain in her head go away.

Everything was so fuzzy. It was as if a hazy fog had settled around her. She had trouble focusing on anything.

"Nancy, can you hear me?"

Nancy wasn't sure where the voice was coming from. She blinked rapidly, hoping the fog would disappear. As things became a little clearer, she realized that Jules was bending over her. He was with two security guards.

"Nancy, can you hear me?" Jules repeated.

She closed her eyes to concentrate and finally managed to speak. "Yes, I hear you. I just feel a little . . . dizzy."

As Jules and the guard helped her to her feet,

Nancy's eyes lit on the cat balloon. Suddenly it all came rushing back to her—the cut rope and . . .

"Someone knocked me out," she said. "The rope. Someone . . ." Her voice trailed off as she saw that the cut ropes had been knotted together.

"Someone cut it," Jules finished for her. "I figured out what had happened when I came back with the guards," he explained. "Luckily we managed to retie the broken ropes before the last one snapped."

Nancy turned to look at the other balloons, then stopped as the throbbing in her head grew worse.

"Don't worry, we already checked the other balloons," Jules said, following her gaze. "The ropes to three other balloons were also cut, but we got to them in time."

Nancy started to ask another question but closed her eyes as her body began to sway. "I think I need some air," she said in a weak voice.

With Jules's help, she grabbed her bag and made her way through one of the huge metal doors and sat down on a bench just outside the entrance. The cold, fresh air made her feel more clear-headed, and Nancy drew in several long breaths. It was still dark out, although the streetlights cut through the deep blackness of the night.

"How long was I out?" Nancy asked Jules, who sat down next to her.

"When I came back with the guards, you were

lying there. I'd say about ten minutes," he answered. He had grabbed a couple of jackets from a pile near the door, and he draped one around her shoulders. "I don't think anyone will mind if we borrow these for a few minutes."

Nancy rubbed her temples and stared down at the frozen patch of ground beneath her feet. She felt so helpless. She knew that the criminal was close by, but he always seemed to be just out of her reach. It was frustrating.

"Nancy, I hope you don't think my dad is responsible for this attack," Jules said, his serious face illuminated by the streetlight above.

"I can't know anything for sure," she said. "He could have cut the ropes before he left. But then, who knocked me out?"

They stopped talking as the Channel Seven news van pulled up next to the curb. A moment later, Aileen Nash hopped out with her camera crew.

"Hi!" Aileen said, her voice bright and cheery. She was wearing a beige suit with a silk blouse that had a fall-colored leaf print on it. "We need to get some early morning shots of everyone getting ready for the parade to show at the start of the telecast. Any great suggestions?"

Nancy looked at her blankly. "Sorry, but I guess getting knocked out has left me too muddled to come up with any creative camera shots," she said.

"What!" Aileen listened as Nancy and Jules

told her about the latest attack on the parade. "Don't worry," Aileen assured them when they were done. "I won't air anything without Jill's say-so. I just hope you find the culprit before something else happens." With that, she headed into the museum with her camera crew.

"I'd better get back inside, too," Jules told her. "Are you sure you're okay?"

"I'm fine. I just need a little more fresh air," Nancy assured him. After he left, she pulled the jacket more tightly around her. It wasn't so much the cold that was getting to her—it was the eerie feeling she had in her bones.

Nancy leaned back on the bench, trying to formulate a plan to catch the saboteur once and for all.

She must have dozed off, because the next thing she knew the sky was growing lighter and her watch read five forty-five. She was shivering, and her feet felt numb, even though she was wearing boots. She stood up and started walking back and forth to warm up. As she did, she looked around. The area around the Museum of Natural History had grown much livelier.

A huge sign that read Clown Corner had been set up next to the museum, at the corner of Seventy-seventh Street and Columbus Avenue. Police barriers had been set up on the side street to block off any nonparade traffic, and dozens of volunteers were already gathering there. From what Nancy could see, they were picking up their costumes in one area and sitting down to have their faces painted in another.

Most of the extras were laughing and squirting their fake flowers at one another. "If they knew what was really going on around here, they might not be so happy," Nancy whispered to herself as she watched them.

The air vibrated with excitement and anticipation. Despite her concern, Nancy couldn't help feeling it, too. The night before, she had made arrangements with Bess to meet her there at six-thirty. Neither of them could stand the thought of Bess missing out on *all* the preparations, regardless of Jill's warning.

Nancy watched as workers began moving floats outside. They took great care in getting each one through the doorway. She was about to go inside and have another look around when Aileen came through the doorway and over to her.

"Feeling better?" Aileen asked. When Nancy nodded, the newswoman said, "We got all of our initial shots, so my crew is taking a short break. Care to join me for some coffee?"

Looking in the direction Aileen indicated, Nancy saw a twenty-four-hour coffee shop across the street. "That sounds perfect," she agreed. "I need something to wake me up. And I'm freezing."

They wove through the crowds to the coffee shop and ordered the hot drinks at the counter.

"So, you still haven't found out who's behind

the sabotage?" Aileen asked as they sat at a table across from a woman reading a fashion magazine.

Seeing Nancy hesitate, Aileen said, "Look, the parade is due to start in just a few hours. I'm not going to air any news of these attacks," she promised. "Besides, at this point, I don't think anything could stop the crowds from showing up."

Aileen was right, Nancy decided. It couldn't hurt to discuss the case with her. Besides, Nancy really needed someone to bounce her thoughts off.

She briefly recapped her suspicions of Louis Clark. "Louis himself couldn't have shown up here, though," Nancy said. "And if he's working with a Mitchell's employee, I still don't have a clue who it is."

Aileen took a sip of her coffee, then asked, "And what's this about Howard Langley? I just saw Jill inside, and she told me *he* might be responsible."

Nancy nodded. "He was here last night. The problem is, we still don't have any proof." She let out a sigh. "I can't help feeling that I'm missing something important."

She reached into her bag and pulled out the thick computer printout. Her eyes scanned the list as she explained to Aileen what it was.

"Hmm, that's funny," Nancy murmured.

"What?" Aileen asked, leaning forward to look at the printout.

For the first time, Nancy had noticed someone whose name never appeared, even though he had been at the warehouse often during the past few days. "It's Neil Steem," Nancy said slowly. "His name should be on this list, but it's not."

"That *is* strange," Aileen agreed.

Nancy blinked as a familiar, sweet scent wafted through the air. She looked to see where it was coming from, and her gaze landed on the woman at the next table. Her magazine was opened to an advertisement announcing the launch of Mitchell's exclusive men's cologne. The woman had unsealed the flap containing a sample of the cologne.

"That's it!" Nancy exclaimed.

Seeing Jill's puzzled gaze, she explained, "The other night Neil was wearing Mitchell's new exclusive cologne. He told me that it's not due to hit the stores until next month, and that he's one of the few people to be wearing it already."

"And?" Jill prompted her.

"And the person who knocked me out this morning was wearing the same cologne. I remember smelling it just before I blacked out." Nancy grabbed the reporter's arm. "Aileen, I think it was Neil Steem!"

Chapter

Thirteen

N ANCY, ARE YOU absolutely sure?" Aileen asked, her eyes wide with surprise.

Nancy nodded. "I remember that smell. And it's definitely the one Neil was wearing when we were at the party at Inverted."

She frowned for a moment before adding, "I suppose it's possible that Howard Langley could have an advance sample of the cologne, too. It's just that I haven't smelled it on him the few times we've met."

A huge smile spread across Aileen's face. "I think I can help you out there," she said. "When Mitchell's first announced the launch of their exclusive perfume and cologne, I covered the story. At the press conference, Howard Langley admitted that he's allergic to cologne and that he could never wear the Mitchell's scent!"

Nancy's mind was racing. "The saboteur *has* to be Neil, then—it all makes sense," she said excitedly. "Neil was with Bess when she bought her scarf. He could have given her the receipt for the clown costumes to sign then. He saw me rush out of the club after her last night, too. He must have guessed that we'd be going to my aunt's, and he made sure to call there before we arrived, knowing that we wouldn't be in the apartment to answer and recognize his voice. Then he went to the warehouse and knocked out the guard and slashed the balloons right before we got there."

Aileen listened in amazement as Nancy pieced the different attacks together. "Neil must have been here last night for the final preparations," she guessed. "He always is. That must be when he cut the balloons. And since he *is* working with the parade, no one would question his presence.

"He even stole a stockboy's ID card so that he couldn't be connected to any of the sabotage attacks," Nancy concluded.

Aileen's expression darkened. "I always knew Neil was bad news," she said. "I guess he thought that if he made Jill look bad, the store's executives would return the parade's top responsibilities to him next year."

"Come on!" Nancy cried, jumping up from the table. "We've got to warn Jill right away. Neil doesn't know we're onto him. For all we know, he could be planning another attack right now!"

By now the floats and balloons were crowding the streets. Nancy and Aileen scanned the crowds for Neil or Jill as they hurried past a balloon of a superhero, his huge cape flapping with the wind. They wound around a float depicting extraterrestrial life, complete with robots that said, "Greetings, Earthlings. Happy Thanksgiving!"

It wasn't going to be easy to tell Jill about Neil, Nancy realized as she hurried toward the Museum of Natural History with Aileen. Jill had believed that he was her friend.

"Where are they?" Nancy said, gazing around. She caught sight of Dan standing by a table of coffee and doughnuts that had been set up.

"Dan, do you know where Jill is?" Nancy asked, after she and Aileen rushed over. "Or Neil?"

"I don't know where Neil is, but last time I saw Jill she was over there." He pointed toward Clown Corner. "Yes, she's still there."

Nancy and Aileen rushed over to find Jill yelling into a portable phone. "What do you mean? Check again!" Jill screamed into the phone. "He *has* to be there!"

Jill looked more distraught than Nancy had ever seen her. But this was too urgent to wait. Glancing down at her watch, Nancy saw that it was already after six-thirty.

"Nancy, I have to get over to my crew," Aileen whispered. "I'll try and get back over here as soon as I can." The newswoman disappeared into the crowd.

Finally, Jill pushed a button and disconnected the portable phone. She began to ask a question, but Nancy interrupted her.

"Do you know where Neil is?" Nancy blurted out.

Jill shook her head. "He was around before," she answered.

"Where is he now?" Nancy persisted.

Jill looked irritated. "If you must know, he had to get more duct tape for one of the floats that's already falling apart. And Austie, the Frisbee-throwing dog, was left behind in the kennel at the hotel, so Neil had to go over and pick him up, too."

Nancy knew not to get offended by Jill's tone. Jill was just overwhelmed with last-minute details. Nancy felt even worse about what she had to tell her. After taking a deep breath, Nancy said, "Jill, I have to tell you something about Neil—"

"Nancy, I'd love to listen, but I've got major problems here," Jill snapped. "And if you hadn't noticed, in a little more than two hours, we're putting on a really big parade. By the way, do you—"

Nancy grabbed Jill's arm. "Jill, I'm almost positive that Neil is the one trying to sabotage the parade!" she said urgently.

In a flash, Jill's expression changed from one of annoyance to one of shock. "What!" she cried.

Nancy explained her theory as quickly as she could, before Jill had time to protest. As she spoke, Jill's face grew red with fury.

"No, I just don't believe any of it," Jill said when Nancy was done. "Neil has been such a big help with everything. He's worked just as hard as I have. There's no way he'd do anything to ruin it."

Jill's voice was trembling, and Nancy thought she saw tears in her eyes. "I just don't believe it, Nancy," Jill said again. "And I don't think you should go around accusing my co-workers, especially on the morning of the parade!"

Nancy faced Jill squarely. She had to get Jill to see the truth. "Jill, on Tuesday Neil left his ID with me by mistake, yet he had no problem getting around the store or the warehouse without it," she began. "I think he's the person who stole Heath Nealon's ID card."

Jill showed no reaction.

"He was around the warehouse before the explosion, so he could easily have planted the timer," Nancy continued. "And the person who knocked me out last night was wearing Forever Male. That cologne isn't even in the stores yet. Neil is the only person I've ever smelled it on."

Jill still didn't seem convinced. In fact, she was

looking impatient, as if she didn't want to hear any of Nancy's argument.

"Neil was also with Bess when she bought her scarf," Nancy said forcefully. "That's the only time Bess signed her name here in New York—which means it's the only time she could have signed for the costumes!"

Finally Jill spoke. "I have one for you, Nancy," she said, her dark eyes flashing angrily. "I've been trying to ask you this since I saw you. Do you know where your friend Bess is?"

Nancy blinked in surprise. What did Bess have to do with any of this? "She was supposed to meet me here at six-thirty. She should be around somewhere," Nancy told Jill.

"Well, believe me, she's not here," Jill said curtly. "I ought to know—I've had Bonnie scouring the area for her or Greg. I'd know it if they were around."

What was going on? Nancy wondered, frowning. "Why are *you* looking for Bess?" she asked.

Jill pressed her lips together in an angry line. "Greg Willow was nowhere to be found when the limousine went to the hotel to pick him up this morning," she explained.

Nancy didn't like the sound of this. "Are you sure?" she asked.

"Positive. I called and talked to every single person who worked at the front desk from five o'clock last night through this morning. Greg dropped off his key at the desk at about five-thirty last night, and he never returned to pick it up."

Jill's voice rose shrilly as she spoke. "In fact" —she was practically shouting now—"the last time anyone saw our grand marshal, he was with your friend Bess!"

Chapter

Fourteen

Nancy felt herself bristle. "You can't think Bess is responsible," she said right away. "She probably slept late, and that's why she's not here yet." She reached into her bag for a quarter. "Let me call my aunt's apartment. I'm sure Bess is there, and we can ask her what happened."

"I already tried that," Jill snapped. "Eloise told me that Bess never came home last night."

"Oh, no!" Nancy knew Bess would never stay out without calling—unless something was terribly wrong. "She must be in trouble," she said, a feeling of dread welling up inside her.

"Jill, we need you over here," Bonnie called from the float line-up. "There's a disagreement about which float Pam Hart is supposed to be on."

Jill waved distractedly at Bonnie before turning back to Nancy. "I don't care what you do about Bess, Nancy. Just please, *please* find my grand marshal so I don't have twenty thousand disappointed teenage girls lined up all the way down Broadway." With that, she turned and went over to Bonnie.

Nancy couldn't stop thinking about Bess. She was filled with worry for her friend as she hurried to a pay phone and dialed her aunt's apartment. She let it ring ten times, but there was no answer. Thinking she might have dialed the wrong number, she hung up and tried again.

"Nancy! Nancy!"

Nancy turned to see her aunt running toward her. "Aunt Eloise!" she called out, rushing to meet her. "What are you doing here?"

"I came right after I got off the phone with Jill," she explained. "I'm so worried about Bess! When she didn't come home last night, I just assumed she had come here to meet you. I'll just feel awful if . . ." Her voice trailed off.

"It's not your fault, Aunt Eloise. But to tell you the truth, I'm worried, too," Nancy confided.

Eloise frowned and shook her head. "Jill seems to think that Bess is responsible for the disappearance of this Greg Willow fellow."

"I think someone else just wants to make it look that way. But since they're both missing, they could be in danger," Nancy said grimly.

"Tell me about last night. When was the last time you saw Bess?"

Nancy's aunt rubbed her cheek. "At about six o'clock," she replied. "Greg picked her up to go out. They said something about stopping at Neil's apartment—"

"To pick up the tickets for the party at the Dot Matrix club!" Nancy finished her aunt's sentence. "Aunt Eloise, come on! We have to get to eighty-eight East Eighty-eighth Street as soon as possible."

"There's the building," Aunt Eloise announced ten minutes later. "Why don't you get out here and I'll park," she said, looking down the street for an open spot.

"Okay," Nancy said. They had driven to the East Side of Manhattan in Eloise's silver hatchback. Now Nancy stepped from the car and walked between two parked cars to the curb.

While she waited for her aunt, Nancy turned to look at the apartment building. She frowned when she spotted a doorman standing behind the glass doors in the lobby.

"All set," Eloise said, coming up to Nancy. She started for the building's entrance, but Nancy held her back.

"There's a doorman," Nancy cautioned.

Her aunt grinned at her. "No problem," she said, shaking her car keys. "I'll tell him I have a problem with my car. When he comes out to help me, you can sneak inside."

Nancy kissed her aunt on the cheek. "That's brilliant!"

"It's no wonder we're related," her aunt said, looking pleased.

Nancy hung back on the sidewalk as her aunt entered the apartment building. A few minutes later, Eloise and the doorman came out and walked past Nancy to the parked car. Nancy waited until they were bent over the engine, and then she slipped inside.

She hurried to the elevator and was relieved when the door immediately opened. Jumping in, she pushed the button for the eighth floor. "Hurry!" she whispered, as if that might coax the elevator to go faster.

Finally, the elevator doors opened on the eighth floor, and she ran down the hallway until she came to apartment 8D. She wasn't surprised to find the door locked. Reaching into her bag, she pulled out the small lock-picking kit she always carried with her and went to work. A few minutes later the lock clicked, and the door swung inward.

She paused briefly, listening for any noise, but there was only silence.

"Bess? Neil?" Nancy called, hurrying into the living room, then the kitchen. There were no immediate signs of Bess and Greg. As she went into the bedroom, Nancy's stomach began to twist with worry.

The room was empty, too, and Nancy went over to the closet door. She opened it—and gasped.

"I knew it!" she whispered.

Dozens of clown costumes were jammed into the closet. That cinched it—Neil was definitely the saboteur. "But where *is* he?" she wondered aloud. "And what's he done with Greg and Bess?"

Nancy took a deep breath, trying to calm herself as she went back into the living room. Think, Drew, she told herself. There must be *some* clue here to where they are.

There were a lot of papers on the coffee table. Sitting down on the sleek black leather couch, she began to flip through them. Most were personal letters and junk mail, but she stopped at an article that had been clipped from a newspaper.

"Historic Building to be Demolished" the headline read.

It was the same story she and Bess had seen Aileen covering, about the brownstone building that was being demolished on Thanksgiving Day. Nancy frowned as she stared down at the newsprint. Why would Neil cut out this article?

A sudden chill ran up Nancy's spine. That building was being demolished *today*. What if Neil had more on his mind than just keeping Bess and Greg out of the way until the parade was over? What if he had a plan to make sure they kept quiet about his scheme—permanently?

Nancy shuddered at the thought. She quickly skimmed the article, but it didn't mention what time the wrecking would start. It was already after seven-thirty. She had to get over there right away!

She flew out the door and back to the elevator. When she reached the ground floor, she tried to act natural and smiled at the doorman as she breezed outside. Then she hurried over to her aunt's silver hatchback and climbed in the passenger seat.

"We have to get to Thirtieth Street and Seventh Avenue!" she said urgently.

As her aunt started the car, Nancy quickly relayed her fears that Bess and Neil were being trapped in the building that was due to be demolished.

"How dreadful!" Eloise gripped the steering wheel more tightly, her eyes trained on the traffic in front of her. "That building is just a few blocks south of the parade route," she said grimly. "So we may have a hard time finding a place to park. We'll probably have to walk a few blocks."

Nancy nodded. "I just hope we get there in time." She pressed her foot against the car floor, mentally urging the car to go faster. All she could think about was Bess and Greg, trapped and fearing for their lives. Nancy didn't think she

136

could ever forgive herself if anything happened to her friend.

"It's not your fault, Nancy," Eloise said, reaching over to pat Nancy's hand. "It's still early. I doubt they would have started wrecking it yet."

Eloise drove downtown on the East Side, then crossed to the West Side on Forty-second Street and headed downtown again. Suddenly she spotted a parking garage with a Vacancy sign outside. "Let's park here," Eloise said. "I think this is the best we can do."

Nancy and Eloise didn't lose a second. They both jumped out of the car, and Eloise left it with the attendant. Then the two of them ran as quickly as they could the last few blocks to Thirtieth Street and Seventh Avenue.

"There it is!" Nancy exclaimed, pointing at the four-story brownstone building.

The area in front of the building, including part of the street, had been blocked off with orange cones and police barriers. About half a dozen men were outside. It looked to Nancy as if they were making some adjustments to their equipment.

"The building's still standing, thank goodness," her aunt said. "Let's go!"

Nancy and Eloise raced past the men, toward the boarded-up entrance.

"Hey! Hey you! You can't go in there!" the foreman screamed after them. "This building's about to be blown up!"

Nancy tried to ignore the shiver that ran through her as she struggled with a board blocking the entrance.

"The timer's set to go off in four minutes! It's locked in—I can't stop it!" the foreman yelled, stalking toward them.

The board finally gave way, and Nancy squeezed inside. Her aunt was right behind her. "Let's split up," Nancy said, trying not to panic. "You take the first two floors. I'll take the top two."

As Nancy raced up the staircase, she heard her aunt calling frantically for Bess and Greg. The wrecking crew was screaming at them on megaphones from outside, too, but she ignored them.

When Nancy got to the third floor, she raced through the rooms, all her senses alert for any sign of Bess or Greg. The windows had been boarded up, so it was difficult to see clearly. The tiny streams of light that came through the slits between the boards only served to cast murky shadows on the walls.

"Bess! Greg!" Nancy was unable to keep the panic from her voice as she scrambled up the last flight of stairs. There were only about two minutes left before the timer was set to go off.

As soon as she reached the hallway, she saw them. Bess and Greg were bound and gagged, and leaning against the wall.

"Aunt Eloise, I found them!" Nancy called,

racing over to Bess and Greg. It took only a few moments to untie the ropes.

"Nancy, I'm so glad you're here!" Bess cried as Nancy removed the piece of tape covering her mouth.

Nancy pulled her friend to her feet. "We have to get out of here. The building's about to blow up!"

The three of them raced down the stairs, picking up Eloise on the second floor. Nancy could still hear the workers screaming at them.

"Thirty seconds!" Eloise shouted.

Nancy was moving so fast that she didn't even feel the steps under her feet as she hurried down the last flight. She made sure the others got through the door. Then she burst outside and rushed toward the street.

She had only gone a few yards when there was a huge boom.

Nancy felt herself being pitched forward. She closed her eyes, covered her head, and rolled to the ground as debris fell all around her!

Chapter

Fifteen

FOR A FEW moments everything around Nancy was in chaos. Then there was silence.

Nancy's heart pounded as she finally lifted up an arm and peeked out. Just ahead of her, her aunt, Bess, and Greg were also lying flat on the ground. Stones and debris were scattered all around them. "Everyone okay?" she asked in a shaky voice.

She was relieved when the others started to dust themselves off and get up. No one appeared to be injured. As Nancy, too, got to her feet, she gazed back at the brownstone they had just escaped from. Where a four-story building had once stood, there was now a pile of rubble.

"I don't know what you crazy people think you're doing!"

Nancy turned to see the foreman heading

toward them, his face purple with rage. A few members of his crew followed behind him.

"You could've been killed in there!" the foreman sputtered. "What in the—" He stopped short, looking back and forth between Bess and Greg. "Where did you two come from?" he demanded.

"I'm sorry we rushed in like that," Nancy said. "Our friends were trapped in the building, and we had to rescue them."

"Trapped! What—?" The foreman wanted to know what was going on.

Nancy looked at her watch. "Sir, we'd love to stay and chat, but we only have forty-five minutes to get this young man to the lead float in the Mitchell's Thanksgiving parade."

The four of them ran, leaving the foreman with a puzzled look on his face. As they hurried back to the parking garage, Bess and Greg explained what had happened.

"After we left the apartment, Greg and I went over to Neil's apartment to pick up the passes for the club," Bess began. "When we walked inside, Neil was his usual self. He offered us some sodas and then went into the kitchen to pour them—"

"There's a cab," Eloise interrupted. "Let's get it. I'll never find a parking space by the museum now. I'll just have to come back for the car later." She hailed the cab, and they all piled in. Nancy's aunt told the driver their destination and asked him to hurry.

As they rode, Bess continued telling what had happened. "Anyway, Neil was gone for a minute, and then he called Greg to the kitchen."

Nancy could guess what had happened next. "You stayed in the living room?" she asked. When Bess nodded, she said, "He separated you so you couldn't gang up on him."

"You got it," Greg said. "I walked into the kitchen, and before I knew it, Neil was swinging something at me, and everything went black." He winced as he rubbed the back of his head.

"I heard a sort of thud, but I just assumed they had dropped something," Bess said, picking up the story. "I mean, this was Neil, Mr. Guest Relations. So when he came out of the kitchen without Greg, I didn't think much of it. I never even saw whatever he hit me with, but I got knocked out, too."

Eloise looked at Greg and Bess. "And when you woke up, you were tied up in that building?"

"Right again," Greg replied. "Neil was still with us. He said he didn't think the wrecking crew would check inside the building as long as there was no sign of anyone tampering with the boards." He let out a bitter laugh. "I guess Neil was very careful because he was right—they never did check."

Bess's voice shook as she exclaimed, "It was awful! Neil even said that if anyone found our . . . our bodies, they would never be able to trace them back to him!"

Nancy was seething with anger toward Neil. How could he hurt her friends like that? Turning in her seat, she saw Bess and Greg exchange glances. She knew they realized they were lucky to be alive.

"I found the clown costumes in his apartment," Nancy told Bess and Greg.

"He told us about that," Greg said. "He actually bragged about how clever he had been to set up Bess to take the blame. When the delivery boy arrived with the costumes, Greg made him wait."

"That's when he met Greg and me to go to Morelli's. He pretended that we were leaving, then suggested that I treat myself to something in the store," Bess explained. "After I signed the receipt, he brought it back to the delivery boy."

Greg shook his head. "We were so busy looking around that we didn't think anything of it when he took off for a minute. The next thing we knew he was back, and we left for Morelli's."

"So I was right about someone putting the delivery receipt on top of your charge receipt," Nancy said. "There were probably a couple of copies of the receipt, and he must have used one of their carbons so your signature would show up on the charge receipt."

Bess nodded, then said, "You were right about his slashing the balloons, too. He had everything planned so well."

"It's scary. He almost got away with it," Greg added, giving the others a meaningful look.

"Not with Nancy Drew on the case!" her aunt said, grinning at Nancy.

A few moments later, the cab pulled up to the curb at Seventy-seventh and Columbus, next to the Museum of Natural History. As they got out of the cab, Greg looked ruefully at his dusty, wrinkled black jeans and button-down shirt. "I hope there's a costume waiting for me here. Nobody's going to want a grand marshal who looks like this."

Bess took his hand and squeezed it. "The fans should just be happy they get to see you at all," she said, smiling up at him.

"Come on, we've got to find Jill and Neil," Nancy said.

As they headed toward Clown Corner, Nancy saw that everything was just about ready. Dozens of clowns in colorful costumes, wigs, and makeup were taking their places in the parade lineup. Floats and bands and balloons stretched down the street in a dazzling line as far as Nancy could see, and the sidewalks were thick with spectators.

"There's Jill!" Eloise called out.

Nancy followed her aunt's gaze and spotted Jill standing between a balloon and a high school band. She looked even more worried and upset than she had earlier—until her gaze landed on the group coming toward her.

"Greg! Where have you been?" she asked frantically. "I've been worried sick."

Greg opened his mouth to explain, but Nancy

cut in. "We'll explain later. Where's Neil?" she asked, looking around.

Jill pointed to the table where coffee was being served. Neil was chatting with a few of the parade guests. Nancy couldn't believe he could act so nonchalant when he had just tried to have Bess and Greg killed.

"You still don't think he was the one trying to sabotage the parade, do you?" Jill asked, eyeing Nancy dubiously.

"I don't *think* so," Nancy told her. "I *know* so! I found the clown costumes in his apartment. *And* he kidnapped Bess and Greg last night."

Jill's eyes flitted nervously to Greg and Neil. Before she could ask any questions, Nancy said, "You'll find out the rest in a minute. Right now, we have to get him."

Nancy was off, leading the group over to the table where Neil was standing. She was still about twenty feet away when he saw them coming toward him.

At first he smiled at Nancy. But when his gaze landed on Bess and Greg, his face went white with shock. He looked nervously around and started to back away, but a group of clowns blocked his way. Some of the clowns thought Neil was trying to joke with them, so they kiddingly blocked his path and squirted water at him from the trick flowers in their lapels.

"Out of my way!" Neil shouted as he tried to get through.

"Give it up, Neil," Nancy called, heading toward him.

Neil shoved a clown out of the way and darted around to the other side of the doughnut table. For the briefest instant, he stared right into Nancy's eyes, and the dark look she saw chilled her to the bone.

Suddenly Neil's hands shot forward, and he grabbed the edge of the table. Nancy gasped as he gave the table a mighty heave, sending it flying right at her!

Chapter

Sixteen

Nancy instinctively dove to the side. She felt something hard strike her foot, then heard the table clatter to the pavement next to her. Cries of alarm rose up from the clowns nearby.

Rolling to her side, Nancy quickly got up. Her foot was sore but didn't seem injured. Doughnuts and coffee cups were scattered on the ground around her.

"Are you all right?" Bess asked with concern. Eloise, Jill, and Greg were right behind her.

Nancy didn't bother to answer. Her attention was focused on Neil, who was running away from her through the crowds. "Stop him!" she shouted, taking off after him.

Within seconds she closed the distance between them. With a final burst of speed, she covered the last few yards and lashed out with a karate kick to Neil's left leg. He fell to his knees with a cry. Nancy quickly grabbed his arm and twisted it behind his back.

A moment later Bess and Greg hurried up with a police officer. "He's the one, Officer," Bess said, pointing at Neil.

"It's no use, Neil," Nancy added, handing him over to the policeman. "We know everything. You were the one who knocked me out last night."

Neil glared at Nancy, but his gaze faltered when he saw Jill. She was looking at him with a mixture of hurt and pity in her eyes.

"Was it really you, Neil?" she asked quietly. "Do you really hate me enough to wreck the parade we both worked so hard for?"

"No, I— It wasn't me!" Neil protested.

"You're lying," Nancy said, shooting him a probing gaze. "You stole Heath Nealon's ID. In fact, I bet you have it right now."

Neil took a step back as the police asked him to empty his pockets. He looked as if he were about to protest. But seeing all the unyielding faces around him, he finally relented.

"My goodness, he *does* have two IDs," Eloise murmured from behind Nancy.

Sure enough, Neil handed over two cards to the police officer. Nancy felt a bubble of triumph when she saw the name *Heath Nealon* on one of them. He also handed over a pocketknife.

"I bet this is what you used to slash the

balloons in the warehouse," Nancy guessed. "And to cut the ropes supporting the helium balloons in the museum last night."

Neil glared at her but said nothing.

"Why me, Neil?" Bess asked, coming over to stand right in front of him. "Why did you try to make it look as if *I* did all those terrible things?"

Neil kicked at the pavement with his shoe before answering. "You set yourself up," he finally said. "I wasn't going to try to pin the sabotage on anyone in particular. But after the explosion, your sunglasses were found near the torches."

"She must have dropped them when I yelled at her to get away from the tanks," Jill put in, "just as you guessed, Nancy."

Nancy nodded but remained silent.

"You were the one who pretended to be Greg and arranged for me to meet him at the parade studio," Bess accused him angrily.

Neil gave her a self-satisfied smile. "That was pretty clever, if I do say so myself. I knew you wouldn't say no to a meeting with Greg at the North Pole, much less Brooklyn. After I called and left a message with Nancy's aunt, I took a cab to the parade studio and waited around the corner until the guard went in to make his rounds. Then I sneaked in, knocked him out, and slashed the balloons. I rigged the door so that it would open for you, then left before you even got there."

Jill had been listening silently to his explanation. Now she asked, "Why, Neil? Why would you do this to me and to the parade? I thought you were my friend."

There was a cold look in Neil's eyes as he gazed at Jill. "I wanted the Mitchell's executives to think that you weren't capable of handling the parade. That way, they would give the responsibility back to me. I deserve to be in charge," he declared angrily. "The parade should never have been taken away from me in the first place."

For the first time, Nancy noticed that Aileen's camera crew had come over and that the camera was rolling. After getting a long shot of Neil's face, Aileen said, "Okay, that's a wrap."

"I'll say," Jill put in wearily. "Officer, take him away." Then she turned to Greg and said, "Come on, we have to get you cleaned up and on the grand marshal's float!"

"Congratulations, Ms. Drew, you saved the parade," Howard Langley said fifteen minutes later. He smiled and extended his hand to Nancy.

"Good job," Jules chimed in.

As Nancy shook Mr. Langley's hand, she looked over at the makeup table where Greg was having some powder brushed on his face. After Neil had been taken away by the police, Nancy, Bess, and Eloise had accompanied Jill and Greg to a wardrobe van. Luckily they had found some slacks and a cowboy shirt that fit Greg. Nancy, her aunt, and Bess had also cleaned up as best they could.

Nancy looked over as Jill emerged from the wardrobe van, handed Greg a cowboy hat, and then came over to Nancy and Bess. "Nancy, how can I ever repay you?" Jill said. "I'm sorry I didn't believe you. I, well—I thought Neil was on my side."

"Don't worry about it," Nancy said, smiling. "I'm just glad everything is all right now."

"And, Bess, I hope you can forgive me for treating you so badly," Jill added, turning to Bess. "I should have believed Nancy when she said you were being set up."

"It's okay. I understand," Bess said. She kept looking around, taking in all the excitement surrounding the parade. "The floats look gorgeous!" she exclaimed. "And look at the great costumes that band is wearing!"

Jill laughed and took Bess's arm. "The least I can do is give you a short tour in the few minutes before the parade begins." She turned to Nancy's aunt and added, "Eloise, why don't you join us?"

As the three of them moved toward the first float, Nancy turned back to Mr. Langley and Jules. "Have you had any luck proving that Louis Clark stole the perfume formula?" she asked.

"Our lawyers presented Louis with all of our evidence and threatened to sue," Mr. Langley explained. "Louis had the brains to see that the millions in legal fees and all of the bad publicity for him and his store would be more trouble than stealing the perfume was worth."

"In other words, he backed off," Jules put in, grinning. "Last night he signed a paper stating that he would not, under any circumstances, duplicate the perfume."

Nancy smiled back at Jules. "Did you ever find out how he managed to duplicate the perfume in the first place?" she asked.

"We can't be sure," Jules replied. "But our lawyers did discover that Louis knows someone who works at the advertising company that's handling the launch of Forever. He must have gotten a sample of the perfume from them and then given it to his scientists to duplicate."

Thinking back, Nancy remembered the sheet of formulas she had found in Louis's desk. "Those vials must have been his scientists' trials," she said. "I bet he broke into the cosmetics lab to try and find a copy of the formula, to see if his scientists had succeeded."

With a shrug, Mr. Langley said, "We may never know for certain. The important thing is that his plan failed, and we have you to thank for that, Nancy."

Nancy could feel herself blush. She was relieved when their attention shifted away from her as Jill, Bess, and Eloise returned.

"I have the perfect idea," Nancy's aunt announced, beaming. "Why doesn't everyone come over to my apartment after the parade for Thanksgiving dinner?"

Howard Langley looked at his son, who replied, "We'd love to! If it's not too much trouble, that is."

Eloise waved dismissively. "It's no trouble at all," she assured him. "I'm going to go downtown and pick up my car, then go home and start cooking. But I'll be watching the parade on TV!"

As Nancy's aunt hurried off, Greg Willow came over from the makeup table. "I hate to break up the party, but it's nine-thirteen, and I've got only two minutes to get to the lead float."

"Over here!" Dan called out, pulling up next to the group in a golf cart. "I'll take you up to the front of the parade, Mr. Willow."

"Come on!" Greg said. He grabbed Nancy and Bess by the hand and started pulling them toward the cart.

Nancy shot Bess a puzzled look. "Where are we going?" she asked Greg.

"You're riding on the lead float with me!"

"We are?" Bess asked.

Pausing to look at Jill, Greg asked, "Is that okay?"

"That's a great idea!" Jill said, giving them the thumbs-up sign.

As Nancy and Bess climbed into the cart with

Greg, they exchanged a look of glee. "We're actually going to ride on the lead float in the Thanksgiving Day parade!" Bess crowed, "George is going to die when she sees us on TV!"

"Here we are," Dan announced a minute later. He stopped the cart next to a float with a huge turkey wearing a top hat. In front of the float a huge banner proclaimed The Forty-first Annual Mitchell's Thanksgiving Day Parade.

The crowd of spectators roared with delight as Greg, Nancy, and Bess got out of the cart and climbed up onto the float. Greg stood in the middle, with Bess to his right and Nancy to the left. No sooner did they start waving to the crowds than the band in front of them burst into a marching song, and the float began to move.

"Not a moment to spare," Greg said, smiling down at Nancy and Bess.

Nancy felt herself being caught up in the excitement of the music and the parade. A plane circled overhead with a banner that read Happy Thanksgiving. In front of them a sea of people stretched as far as the eye could see. Nancy caught a glimpse of Aileen and her crew filming the event.

Glancing over at Bess, Nancy saw that she was grinning from ear to ear. She and Greg were both waving to the crowds.

"Happy Thanksgiving, Bess," Nancy said, leaning close to her friend.

Bess's eyes shone as she gave Nancy a hug. "Same to you, Nan. This is the best Thanksgiving ever!"

She and Bess smiled at each other. Then they turned and waved to the crowds.

Nancy's next case:

Someone's out to deep-six WRVH-TV anchorman Hal Taylor. A series of death threats directed at handsome Hal have put the entire station on edge. The solution: Bring Nancy Drew on board to work undercover as an investigative reporter. She'll be in the perfect position to get the inside story on who wants to cut Taylor out of the picture.

Nancy finds the evening news to be full of violence, ambition, and greed—and that's just *behind* the camera, on the set. Taylor's the star of the show, an easy target, and Nancy knows that more than his career is in danger. If she doesn't break the story soon, the lead on tomorrow's newscast could be "Murder at WRVH" . . . in *UPDATE ON CRIME,* Case #78 in the Nancy Drew Files™.